erilaR

Part IV

The

Iron One

erilaR

Part IV

The

Iron One

by

Hector Miller

www.HectorMillerBooks.com

erilaR

Part IV

The Iron One

All characters and events in this publication, other than those clearly in the public domain, are fictitious and any resemblance to real persons, living or dead, is purely coincidental.

Author: Hector Miller

Proofreading: Kira Miller

First edition, 2022, Hector Miller

Part 4 in the book series erilaR

ISBN: 9798372072626

Text copyright © 2022 CJ Muller

All rights reserved.

No part of this publication may be reproduced, stored in a retrieval system, or transmitted, in any form or by any means, without the prior permission in writing of the author. Publications are exempt in the case of brief quotations in critical reviews or articles.

Contents

Chapter 1 – Guest (May 474 AD) 1

Chapter 2 – Hunt 10

Chapter 3 – Lamb 18

Chapter 4 – Wolf (June 474 AD) 27

Chapter 5 – Black Gold 34

Chapter 6 – Svear 42

Chapter 7 – White wind 51

Chapter 8 – Hrothgar 59

Chapter 9 – Mead hall 68

Chapter 10 – Champion 76

Chapter 11 – Arm 86

Chapter 12 – Shingle 94

Chapter 13 – Message 102

Chapter 14 – Burichai (July 474 AD) 111

Chapter 15 – Kurs 120

Contents (continued)

Chapter 16 – Boat 129

Chapter 17 – Thirteenth tribe 137

Chapter 18 – Smola 145

Chapter 19 – Kyiv 153

Chapter 20 – Do not sleep 161

Chapter 21 – Coward 171

Chapter 22 – Oath 179

Chapter 23 – Baian 190

Chapter 24 – Birds (September 474 AD) 198

Chapter 25 – Trust 207

Chapter 26 – Child (October 474 AD) 214

Chapter 27 – Power 222

Chapter 28 – Zeno 232

Chapter 29 – Gold (December 474 AD) 245

Chapter 30 – Mob 257

Contents (continued)

Chapter 31 – Sagum 266

Chapter 32 – Rhodos (February 475 AD) 276

Chapter 33 – Burden 288

Chapter 34 – Italia (March 475 AD) 300

Chapter 35 – Arrangement 312

Historical Note – Main Characters 325

Historical Note – Storyline 329

Historical Note – Random Items 335

Historical Note – Place Names 341

erilaR – The Iron One

"Ride the horse did the bold champion, chief of men, over the shores of the Hraiðsea. Now he sits armed on his steed, his shield strapped, foremost of the famous."

- Extract from a translation of the Rök Runestone.

Chapter 1 – Guest (May 474 AD)

The ringfort of the Heruli in the land of the Svear.

Present day Herrhamra, Sweden.

Abdarakos took a deep swallow from his drinking vessel then wiped his silver beard with the back of his free hand.

Deep in thought, he rhythmically tapped the gilded tip of the empty horn on the rough-hewn oak of the table, no doubt thinking on the words of our guest. Although the grizzled war leader had seen nearly sixty summers, the muscles bulged underneath the multitude of warrior bands adorning his upper arms, and the sinews still rippled across his corded forearms.

Eventually he drew a deep breath and slowly exhaled. His gaze settled on Othere, the king of the Svear.

"No", he growled. "My answer is no."

The dull orange glow from the embers in the hearth provided sufficient light for me to notice that the young king's cheeks had turned a darker shade of red. It was clear that my grandsire's words angered him, but Othere was not fool enough to gainsay the man who had once commanded the armies of the great khan, Attila.

"May I ask why?" Othere said.

Abdarakos did not offer a reply immediately, but regarded Othere like a viper would its prey.

"When one is in need of plunder, it is never a good idea to ravage the house next door", the erilar growled. "Because when you leave your home and venture into the forest to hunt, your neighbour will have his vengeance and take his blade to your family."

"But the Svear and the Gautar have been raiding each other's lands for as long as anyone can remember", Othere replied, his tone almost pleading.

"And what do the Svear gain from these excursions, boy?" Abdarakos growled.

All knew that it was the Heruli who wielded the true power in the land, and Othere, who owed his crown to Abdarakos, chose wisely to ignore the deliberate insult.

"Slaves, women, ale and cattle", the king replied. "Sometimes even horses."

"Which you forfeit later in the season when the Gautar raid your lands in turn", Abdarakos sneered. "The Svear and the Gautar are like two old women who keep going back and forth, stealing each other's only chicken."

The expression on Othere's face hinted at the fact that he was starting to lose control over his emotions. Concealed from my grandsire's view, the king's hand settled on the hilt of his dagger, which he slowly drew from its fur-lined sheath.

"You have grown old and fear the Gautar", Othere hissed while baring his blade.

Abdarakos lunged across the table. His left hand moved faster than the eye could see and caught the king's wrist in a vice-like grip. "The wolf warriors have come to this land because the gods willed it so", the erilar growled, and gestured at me with his chin. "Already the blood of the Heruli is mixing with that of the Svear. Together we will become a great people."

But honeyed words had never been the way of the great man. He reached out with his right hand, closed his fist around the embroidered weave adorning the king's chest, and pulled him closer, hauling him across the oak. Then the erilar tightened his grip of steel and the dagger clattered onto the stone floor. "Dare show me the iron of your blade again", he growled, his voice like the keel of a longboat grating on shingle, "and I will rip your head from your shoulders and feed it to the hogs."

My grandsire released the ashen king, leaned over to retrieve the dagger, and gave it back, hilt first. "Sit, King Othere", he said. "Let us share another horn of ale and I will tell you what I have in mind."

Dutifully I stood and extended my hand to Othere, who handed me his gilded vessel. I dipped it into the large clay jar and passed the brimming horn back to the king. I repeated the process for Abdarakos and finally for myself before retaking my seat.

The erilar grunted his thanks and took a long draught of the golden liquid.

"Send messengers to all the towns and hamlets", Abdarakos said. "Gather the young men who yearn for adventure and treasure. There will be many who will answer your call, lord king."

"I will test them and choose the best, three hundred in all. I will load them onto my longships and toughen their sinews at the oars on our journey to the lands of Rome. Tribune Flavius Odovaker, who leads the armies of Italia, will teach them the way of the sword and the spear."

"And how will it benefit the Svear?" Othere asked. "It seems that the armies of Rome will be bolstered at the expense of my people."

"The Empire does not send its warriors into battle half-naked like the Svear and the Gautar", my grandsire replied. "Roman gold will pay for arms and armour crafted from iron. And the purses of our young men will soon bulge with the coin of their defeated enemies."

"Many will die", Othere said. "And the Svear will be a weakened people."

Abdarakos chugged the remainder of his ale and handed the horn to me for a refill.

"That is true, lord king", he said. "Many will perish in the endless wars of the Empire. But the ones who return to this land will be battle-hardened men – corpse-makers of renown. They will be clad in iron from head to toe and their arming belts will bristle with swords, axes and daggers forged from the best iron that coin can buy. One such veteran is worth more than half a dozen screaming, half-naked Gautar."

Abdarakos had earlier told me to dress in the armour of the excubitors, the elite guards of the Eastern Emperor.

The reason became evident as he gestured at me. "How many of your men will you send against my grandson, Ragnar, lord king? Four, five … mayhap seven?"

Othere regarded my polished armour of iron mail, scale and boiled leather for a span of heartbeats. Then his eyes settled on my bearded axe that lay on the table beside me.

"I see what you mean, war leader", the king said, his gaze fixed on the honed edge of the magnificent blade.

My grandsire fumbled in his pocket and produced a gold *solidus* which had been pierced and attached to a leather thong. He handed the coin to the king, who flipped the newly minted piece between his fingers.

"A gift to seal our agreement", Abdarakos said, then raised his drinking vessel in a toast.

The king reciprocated.

"To warriors clad in iron and purses bulging with gold", the erilar growled, and all three of us downed the contents of our horns.

* * *

Unni leaned over the iron pot and used a copper ladle to heap generous helpings of wheat and barley porridge into our wooden bowls.

"If we wish to cross the passes before the snow comes, we will have to brave the Austmarr before the end of July", Kursik said, nodded his appreciation to my wife, and used his dagger to scoop a dollop of butter onto the steaming porridge.

I nodded my agreement with the Hun's words, and poured buttermilk onto the hot food before sweetening it with forest honey.

"Will we row up the Oder to the lands of the Heruli?" he asked.

"The erilar told me that he plans to travel with us", I said, and took a swallow of mead. "My uncle, Mourdagos, will also be sending men to bolster the ranks of Prince Ottoghar's forces. The Boat Lord's longships will take us down the Elbe, I suppose."

Just then, Boarex, the hulking Hun, strolled into my hall, a frown of irritation creasing his brow. His horn bow was in his right fist and he gripped a full quiver in the other.

"Where is the Goth?" Kursik asked, referring to our friend Beremud.

I gestured to the back of the hall from where rhythmic snoring could be heard emanating from underneath a heap of furs. "Ale", I said, by way of explanation. "He emptied the barrel, and the batch that Unni brewed will only be ready next week."

"A few days without ale will do him good", Kursik said.

"I thought that his woman would sort him out", Boarex mused. "He was supposed to come by the warrior hall at first light. It is our turn to hunt for the pot."

"I'm afraid to say it, but I believe that Maela is not helping at all", I said. "On the contrary, it would be safe to say that she is encouraging his bad habits."

Unni reached out and pinched my arm, soliciting a yelp. "That's for being mean to your friend", she said. "You two are just jealous", she added. "Maela is a good woman who dotes on Beremud."

Beremud, who undoubtedly had a way with the fairer sex, had become acquainted with the girl in Gaul during the aftermath of our defeat at the hands of Euric, the Visigoth King. Shortly after we had returned home, they tied the knot. Unni, who had struck up a friendship of sorts with Maela, was the one who insisted that we take the two newlyweds in under our roof until they could build a place of their own.

At that moment Maela walked into the hall.

"Greetings", she said when she noticed Boarex, who acknowledged her with a nod.

The dark-haired Maela, who carried a brimming horn, walked over and crouched down beside the heap of furs. She reached out and gently stroked Beremud's arm until the snoring subsided. Moments later, a head, topped with a mop of unruly hair, appeared.

"Love", Maela said softly, kissed her man on the cheek, and pushed the horn into his hand. "Have some ale to clear your head. I noticed the leafy branch above the neighbours' door this morning and went to get this for you."

I raised an eyebrow and stole Unni an I-told-you-so glance.

Unni's hands went to her hips – a sure sign that I was in trouble.

But before my wife was able to offer a retort, Kursik gained his feet. "Come", he said. "If we don't leave now there will be no meat to add to the pottage tonight."

Chapter 2 – Hunt

When the undergrowth became too dense to continue on horseback, we tethered our mounts to the moss-covered trunk of a long-fallen alder. Kursik and Boarex's feet had hardly touched the ground when they reached for their horn bows. I always felt naked without my axe, so I took it from the saddle, reached behind my back, and pushed the haft of the bearded weapon into the sheath attached to the rear of my mail shirt. Only then did I take my bow into my fist.

Beremud, who was still plagued by the aftereffects of the ale, left his unstrung bow tied to the saddle and reached for his heavy hunting spear, which was tipped with a leaf-shaped iron head.

"I will take you to the place where I last saw the tracks of wild boar", Boarex whispered and melted into the underwood.

We were all accomplished hunters, and followed the Hun, making sure to move with stealth.

For two miles Boarex led us along ravines overgrown with ferns and across forested hills dense with alder, beech and oak. Eventually he raised a hand, crouched down, and gestured for us to approach. The Hun carefully parted the shrubs obscuring our view, and indicated where a grove of ancient oaks stood on a stretch of flat ground. It was too early in the season for acorns, but sixty paces ahead, a dozen wild boar of all sizes were snorting contently, foraging for roots and worms.

Kursik issued a grin and clasped Boarex's shoulder.

The two Huns and I reached for our quivers, all opting for hazel wood shafts tipped with broad-bladed iron heads. I nocked, and exhaled slowly as I drew the sinew string back. My gaze remained focused on the spot where my arrow would strike, a handspan behind a large male's ear.

Before we released, one of the pigs issued a grunt of alarm. Within the blink of an eye the boar scattered into the underwood. Moments later, there followed a series of bloodcurdling squeals – and then there was complete silence – devoid of even the usual calls of partridges and hoots of grouse.

We exchanged glances.

"Something, or someone, killed those boar", Boarex hissed softly.

"Hunters?" Kursik suggested.

"Who of the Svear will dare hunt in the forests of the erilar?" Beremud asked.

I slipped the hunting arrow back into the quiver and took two shafts tipped with armour-piercing iron into my draw hand. Both Huns followed suit.

With arrows nocked and strings drawn back, we made our way across the open ground underneath the giant oaks. By the time we reached the thicket into which the boar had disappeared, the silence had lifted and the usual sounds of the forest had returned.

We searched the area for long, but found no evidence of violence until Kursik beckoned us, whistling like a snow jay.

We found the Hun crouching at the perimeter of a trampled area speckled with drops of bright blood. He leaned forward and used the tip of his dagger to spear a piece of discarded offal, which he studied with interest, turning the dagger to look at it from all sides.

"It is the remains of a swine's heart", he said, and used his forefinger to indicate where human teeth had torn away at the still-warm flesh.

* * *

Runa listened intently, a frown furrowing her brow.

"Whoever killed the boar left no tracks", I said, confirming Kursik's words. "And the carcasses of the swine seem to have vanished into thin air."

"Fill my horn with sweet mead if you wish to hear a tale", the old woman said. She lowered herself onto the soft furs beside the hearth fire and gestured for us to join her.

"It happens when the gods send the *vargavinter* to the ice forests of the north", she hissed, and even the flickering flames seemed to retreat before her words, cowered by her fierce countenance.

"When the wolf winter creeps down from the north, the reindeer and the snow rabbit scatter before the icy breath of the frost giants. Flesh eaters like the sea bear and the white fox leave their usual hunting grounds to seek out a place where they can feast on prey. And so do the *creatures who have no name.*"

We were all familiar with the northern hunters who travelled south during their harsh winters to trade seal pelts and horse-whale tusks for Svear iron.

"The *Sami*?" I asked.

Runa issued a dismissive grunt, took a swig from her horn, and swirled the sweet liquid in her mouth before swallowing - all the while fixing me with a glare I had seen mothers use on ignorant children.

As I expected, Runa did not dignify my question with an answer.

"The last time *the nameless ones* came to the lands of the Svear was sixty moons ago, when I was but a young maiden", she said. "At first our warriors returned empty-handed, telling strange tales of wounded animals that had vanished without leaving tracks. Later, hunters ventured into the woods never to return."

Runa paused for a moment and stretched out an open palm to soak up the heat of the fire, then took another swallow to wet her throat.

None around the hearth dared interrupt the old seer.

"Soon there were rumours about a terrible evil that had been unleashed on the clan", she croaked. "Some claimed to have glimpsed creatures in the forest, *draugar* that were half-man, half-wolf. Others ridiculed them, convinced that someone in the village had offended the gods. We made sacrifices to appease the old deities until the mud of the streets turned red with blood."

"Then our livestock that grazed near the edge of the trees started to disappear", she whispered. "Soon we were too scared to take the cows and goats to pasture."

"It was the day after the first child had been taken that the elders wished for my mother to travel to the realm of the heavens and converse with the gods", she said. "At dawn the next morning I ventured into the greenwood to collect the mushrooms and herbs my mother required."

Runa took a sip from her horn and her gaze focused somewhere in the glowing embers while she searched her memory. Suddenly her face contorted with an expression of fear and she took a deep breath to calm herself.

"At first I thought it was a wolf feeding on a kill", she said. "But then the corpse-pale creature raised its head, sniffed the air, and reluctantly tore itself away from the carcass of the red deer it had been feasting on. Slowly it turned its gaze on me, bright blood still dripping from its lips. Then it stood up onto its hind legs."

"By the gods", Kursik whispered, and reached for his wolf's paw amulet, his eyes wide.

"It came at me then, and I knew that I could not escape it", Runa said. "I stumbled backwards, against the trunk of an oak, and made my peace with the gods."

"But it was not my time. A pack of wolves, no doubt attracted by the blood of the creature's kill, came growling from the darkwood and fell upon the vile apparition."

"I slid down into the cover of the ferns and remained there for almost half the morning, too afraid to draw more than shallow breaths, never mind move or utter a sound. When the wolves had had their fill of the flesh of the red deer, they returned whence they came. Eventually I walked over to the ravaged remains of the human body, only to find that the savage creature had been a woman."

Unni issued a gasp of surprise. "Did you tell the villagers?" she asked.

"I was young, but not a fool, child", she sneered at Unni. "Who would have believed me?"

"I told my mother of the happenings, and later, before evening came, I led her to the place where the wolves had killed the woman, but nothing remained – not even a drop of blood on the carpet of leaves."

"And then the season turned", she said with a shrug. "Boar, red deer and elk were again seen in the forest and people moved on with their lives. Once again our huntsmen returned with fresh meat when they ventured into the greenwood. The villagers soon forgot, choosing to believe that we had been terrorised by a pack of wolves that had come down from the north."

Runa leaned in and lowered her voice. "Have a care, warriors", she said. "The *ones whose have no name* have returned to the land of the Svear."

Chapter 3 – Lamb

Abdarakos sat cross-legged on the furs and used the blade of his dagger to slice bite-sized strips of dried beef from a larger cut. Chewing steadily, he popped the thin slices into his mouth while he listened to my words.

Two paces away, Sigizan, who had taught me the way of the horse and the bow, stood leaning against an oak post, munching on hard cheese. The Hun champion shared the hall with the shaman and the erilar.

"I have heard tales of a strange people who dwell in the lands to the north", Atakam said. "Their skin is corpse-pale and their hair white as snow. Like wolves, they follow the herds they prey upon and give no heed to boundaries set by man. They do not till the earth, nor do they keep sheep, goats, cattle or horses. Apart from a bow and a bundle of furs, they have no earthly possessions and neither do they covet silver, gold or treasure."

"Who are they?" Sigizan asked.

"They have no name", the old shaman replied.

"I do not fear the tales of old women", the erilar growled. "Tomorrow we will ride out and drive these base creatures from the lands of the Heruli. If a wolf is able to kill them, so can we."

"If you can find them", Atakam replied.

* * *

The following morning, twenty warriors rode out through the thick timber gates at the hour of the wolf, the grey time before dawn, when the raven-god sends out his birds across middle earth.

Abdarakos led us into the dark wood. We rode in near silence, the sound of our horses' hooves masked by the thick carpet of leaves.

But our excursion soon proved to be futile. Not for a heartbeat did we lay eyes on the creatures we sought. Once, our horses' ears pricked up and we charged into the undergrowth, but found not even as much as a footprint.

By mid-afternoon the erilar reined in and turned his horse's head back in the direction whence we came. "The old shaman was right", he growled. "It is like chasing *draugar* in fog. We are wasting our time."

The sun was about to dip below the western horizon when we eventually arrived before the walls of the ringfort. The fact that the gate was closed hinted that all was not well.

Haldr, the red-haired Svear who had fought in the armies of Rome, appeared on the wall walk above the entrance and ordered his men to lift the locking bar.

Abdarakos spoke to the Svear while the heavy oak doors creaked open. "Come to my hall", he said to the redheaded warrior. "I am tired and thirsty. You will tell me what troubles you while we share a horn of ale."

Not long after, Haldr joined Abdarakos, Sigizan, Atakam and me around a blazing fire in my grandsire's hall.

The erilar commanded a thrall to fill our horns, and took his place beside the hearth. Once all of us had wetted our throats, Abdarakos nodded to the Svear – a sign that he could tell us of the day's happenings.

"Early this morning, not more than two hours after you left, one of the children who tends to the animals came running towards the gate, screaming", he said. "Three goats were feeding close to the treeline, the child said. One moment they were still grazing, the next moment they had disappeared."

"And he did not see the goat thieves", Abdarakos ventured, "nor could you find their tracks."

Haldr's shoulders slumped. "I took ten men into the forest, lord", he said. "Men who know the way of the greenwood. But we could find … nothing."

"They are more like beasts than men", Sigizan said.

Then an idea came to me.

"If they are like animals, why not hunt them like animals?" I asked. "How do hunters kill troublesome wolves?"

"I was but a boy when I rode out with my father to tend to our herds", Sigizan said. "A pack had overwhelmed the herd dogs and killed more than a hundred of our sheep in a single night. They had not killed because of hunger but they ravaged the flock to sate their lust for blood."

"I recall seeing tears in my father's eyes as he slit the throats of the ewes and lambs that still lived after being ravaged by the beasts. The wolves had not killed them outright. With their powerful jaws they had crushed the sheeps' legs or severed their spines. When their prey were unable to flee, the predators ripped open their stomachs to feast on their livers."

"In a nearby ravine we found a lamb that had somehow managed to escape the slaughter. My father tied the poor animal between two stakes near a rocky outcrop where we waited in ambush."

"I still remember the desperate bleating of the lamb when the wolves came", Sigizan said. "We killed ten that night, and the ones we wounded we rode down the following day."

"Then that is how we will hunt the hunters", I said.

"With a lamb?" Haldr asked, no doubt confused.

"I will be the lamb", I replied.

"What happened to the staked sheep?" Abdarakos asked Sigizan as an afterthought.

"The wolves killed it, of course", the Hun said, and chugged what remained of his ale.

* * *

That evening, when the sun had set and a sickle moon rose in the east, Kursik and Boarex slid across the wooden wall of the fort. They moved in the shadows of the rampart and then kept close to the stone wall that separated the pastures from the fields as they made their way towards the woods.

The two Huns had exchanged their iron armour for furs, and we had darkened their hands and faces with soot from the hearth.

Abdarakos rested his hand on my shoulder while I squinted into the thin moonlight. "Go to your furs, Ragnar", he said. "Tomorrow will be a long day."

I nodded my agreement, walked towards my hall, and slid in underneath the furs beside Unni.

* * *

I felt a cold skeletal hand grip my shoulder. "Wake up, brave warrior", Runa croaked, and I could not help but discern the mocking tone hidden somewhere in her words.

Before I could offer a retort, she made her way to Beremud and his woman, and kicked my friend's leg. "You, too, Goth", she screeched, and issued a cackle.

Unni helped me to strap on my armour. The old seer shuffled over to the meal-fire and ladled generous scoops of fish, root and ale broth into two large wooden bowls.

While Beremud and I were emptying the bowls, Runa bent down and stroked the ears of the large brown dog that was lying in its usual place close to the fire. Outside, somewhere in the hills, we heard the howl of a wolf.

Runa looked up from scratching the hound and her eyes met mine. "In days long past, man and wolves were at odds, like they still are", she said. "But someone, inspired by the gods, had the courage to tame them."

I nodded absentmindedly, paying the old seer little heed.

But Runa reached out and grabbed my wrist in a surprisingly strong grip. "Hear my words, Ragnar", she growled. "The wolf can be tamed."

I nodded, this time looking her in the eye, and she released my hand. But I had other things on my mind and the words of the seer were soon forgotten.

We had hardly finished our breakfast when we heard the sound of hooves. I kissed Unni on the cheek, took my bow and quiver, and made my way to the back of the hall where the animals were kept.

Outside in the street, Abdarakos and his oathsworn were waiting for us, mounted and ready to ride.

"Come", the erilar said. "Let us go and tether the lamb."

* * *

We had travelled more than four miles into the greenwood when Abdarakos signalled that we should rest, water the horses, and take repast.

We all dismounted. When I was shielded by the other riders from any eyes that could be watching from the shadows, I pressed a short nail into the hoof of my mare, rubbed her muscular neck, and asked her for forgiveness in advance.

Three hundred heartbeats later, I swung up into the saddle and followed Abdarakos and Sigizan, who led the way deeper into the forest. We had hardly gone to a trot when my horse protested and refused to put weight on one of its legs.

Abdarakos raised a hand and the whole column came to an abrupt halt.

I slid from the saddle and Sigizan followed suit.

We inspected the horse's hoof and Sigizan raised both his palms and shook his head vigorously – just like we had rehearsed. To someone watching from the shadows it was clear that my horse was in no condition to continue.

Abdarakos ordered two of his ringmen to return to the village to bring a spare horse. Then they bade me farewell and continued deeper into the woods.

The lamb had been tethered.

Chapter 4 – Wolf (June 474 AD)

As there was no need for my mare to suffer further, I removed the iron nail from her hoof with a flick of my dagger and received a whinny that I chose to take as a sign that I had been forgiven.

I tied my horse to a branch and sat down close by, making myself comfortable against the trunk of an ancient ash.

Abdarakos had not been gone long when a deathly silence descended over the forest.

I stood, strapped on my riveted iron helmet, and slowly slipped my bearded axe from its sheath on my back.

Fifty paces ahead, the undergrowth stirred.

For a long moment I thought that I had imagined it, but then the ferns and saplings shuddered as something large, still concealed within the thicket, slowly but deliberately made its way towards me.

Again, I spied movement in the shrubbery, this time to my left. My right fist tightened around the ashwood and I slid my left hand closer to the butt, angling the haft across my body, the blunt end of the blade facing the threat.

A primal roar erupted from the underwood. Less than a heartbeat later a massive bear burst from the thicket and attacked. I thrust the haft of my axe into its gaping jaws, but only stalled it for a moment before the beast lashed out at me with its four-inch-long claws. The powerful swipe tore the scales from my armour, and were it not for the iron breastplate underneath, it would have ripped open my ribcage.

I staggered backwards and the bear came in for the kill. But two three-bladed Hun arrows slammed into the beast's shoulder, making it bellow in pain. It was only distracted for a moment before it turned its attention back to me. A heartbeat later, two more arrows sprouted from its side.

Kursik and Boarex had expected to use their shafts on unarmoured warriors, and the light hunting arrows that could easily pierce the torso of a man failed to penetrate the thick fur and tough hide of the bear.

Again, my Hun friends released a volley of arrows and the bear turned on them.

The appearance of the beast had caused me to forget about the movement I had earlier noticed to my left. At that moment a fur-clad shape materialised from the shadows, five paces away.

At first I believed it to be a wolf, but the creature came erect and swiped at me with what appeared to be a bone-hafted dagger fitted with a crude blade crafted from stone. With contempt I took the swipe on my boiled leather vambrace. Almost immediately I felt the familiar sting and I realised that somehow the dark blade had managed to cleave the leather and draw blood.

I studied the man-creature who circled me, his dagger at the ready. His face, beard and hair were corpse-pale and his eyes white with a blueish hue. His arms and legs were bound with furs and his torso covered by a wolfskin tunic.

He lunged again, and this time I respected the weapon and skill of the wild man who wielded it. I took the blow on the wood my axe, slid my right hand along the haft, closer to the butt, and brought the head around in a chopping motion. The man was quick, but I was faster, and the iron of the honed edge of the blade brushed his forearm, cut through the furs, and scored a bloody line along his skin.

A roar came from the right where I had last seen the two Huns battling the bear. From the corner of my eye I noticed that Boarex lay sprawled on the forest floor, unmoving. I saw the crazed animal, riddled with arrows, take a swipe at Kursik who was defending his prone friend. But the Hun lost his footing and fell heavily, coming to a rest beside Boarex.

I roared a challenge at the beast. The bear, having dealt with the Huns, turned to face us. It shook its great head, reared up onto its hind legs, then cantered towards us, no doubt wishing to eliminate what it perceived as the remaining threat.

I turned to confront the animal, but stole a glance at the wild man and noticed that he was also facing the onrushing beast.

It could have been my imposing armour or the shine of my helmet, but I believe that it was the intervention of the gods. For whatever reason, the animal chose to ignore me and turned on my foe.

With the agility normally reserved for feral creatures, the hunter dodged a swipe that would have crushed his skull. He avoided the terrible jaws and buried his knife up to the hilt in the bear's neck.

It helped him naught.

The beast charged into the wild man, who fell heavily onto his back. The bear gripped a fur-covered arm and shook the man like I have seen a dog shake a troublesome rat.

That was the moment I chose to strike. I ran at the animal, whose attention was focused on its prey, and the head of my axe came around in an almighty swing. The flat of the blade struck the bear against the side of the head and caved in its skull. For a moment in time the beast swayed on its feet, then collapsed on top of the prone man.

Only a fool leaves an enemy alive when the gods provide an opportunity, so I hefted my axe above my shoulder to take the wild man's head.

I felt a strange presence, and mid-swing, the words of Runa came to me. *'Remember, Ragnar, the wolf can be tamed.'*

The axe came around and the blade bit deep into the soft soil beside the hunter's head. The wild man, who had stared at me defiantly, closed his eyes and issued a sigh. Over and over, he mumbled a phrase in a tongue that sounded both foreign and familiar. "*Man van yster. Man van yster.*"

I pulled the iron free of the soil and made my way to Kursik and Boarex who were coming to. Just then I heard the clopping of hooves and noticed Abdarakos returning with his oathsworn. Almost simultaneously the rider who had gone to the village arrived back, accompanied by Atakam.

The shaman kneeled beside the injured Huns and inspected their wounds. "Boarex won't ride or draw a bow for at least two moons", the healer croaked, drawing a groan from the Hun. "Kursik will walk with a limp for long", he said. "Not that it matters", Atakam added, "as he rarely walks."

Abdarakos, who was still in the saddle, steered his horse to where the hunter was still trapped underneath the bulk of the bear. The erilar hefted his spear and I had no doubt that he was about to do that which I had left undone.

To my surprise Atakam hobbled over to the war leader's side and whispered words.

My grandsire issued a grunt of acknowledgement, lowered his spear and commanded his ringmen, "Bind the wolfman's hands and take him to the hall of Ragnar".

"And slaughter the beast", he added. "Tonight, we will feast on the flesh of the bear."

A great cheer erupted from amongst his oathsworn.

* * *

"He said his name is Auvokauko", Runa said while she pressed the crushed herb paste into the deep cuts on the wolfman's chest where the claws of the bear had ripped through his furs. "But his people call him Kauko."

"How do you know his words, grandmother?" Unni asked.

"Like me, my grandmother was the medicine woman of our clan", Runa said. "She taught me the language of the ancients, the tongue that the gods gave to man. The tongue of the Svear has changed much since then, but Kauko's people have remained uncorrupted, close to the Mother, true to the ways of the ancient gods."

"Will he live?" I asked Runa.

"Do I look like a god to you?" the old woman sneered.

"If the gods heal him, how long will it take?" I asked, rephrasing the question.

"He will be ready on time", Runa said, her tone dismissive. "Now go and play with your axe, warrior", she growled, bidding me to leave her to her toil.

Chapter 5 – Black Gold

The predations of the unnamed hunters came to an end as suddenly as it had started.

Ten days later, Runa declared that Kauko's wounds had sufficiently healed and that he no longer required her ministrations.

"He must be allowed to return to his people", Runa declared while she watched her patient slurp chicken broth from a wooden bowl. "If he wants to", she added in a near whisper.

"He attacked me", I said, and immediately regretted uttering the words that, to my own ears, sounded like the whining of a petulant child.

Kauko, despite the fact that his kind was akin to beasts, possessed a mind as sharp as his black obsidian blade. Within days he had picked up on enough words of the Svear language to carry a simple conversation.

He slapped his muscular chest. "Kauko stay", he proclaimed.

Runa nodded, but the wild man deferred to me, waiting on my answer.

The last thing I wished for was to have a guest in my hall, particularly one who had tried to open my throat. I shook my head. "You must return to your kind", I said.

Kauko regarded me with his near white eyes and nodded. "I do what you say, Iron One."

The following morning when I woke, I found that our guest had departed during the night. It was no surprise that none of us had noticed. We were all well aware of the wolfman's capacity for moving with stealth.

"I sense that the thread of his life is somehow entwined with yours, Ragnar", Runa declared while she scooped porridge into my bowl later that morning. "You should not have allowed him to go. Kauko believes that the Earth Mother, the one we call Nerthus, spared his life so that he could serve you. He told me that he has dreamed it, that he would serve the Iron One."

"Why did you not tell me sooner?" I asked.

"I am not your mother, warrior", she growled. "I serve the gods."

There was no point in continuing the conversation with the old seer. I had sent Kauko away and even if I wished it, I would never find him – or so I thought at the time.

* * *

On the morrow, Abdarakos received a missive from the Svear king. Othere informed the war leader that he had managed to gather three hundred young men and that they would arrive at Runaville within the week.

Later that morning, I accompanied my grandsire to the shore where he inspected the beached hulls of our longships that had recently been scraped clean of the growth of the sea. From time to time he paused to take a closer look and ran a practised hand across the surface of the timber, showing me the telltale signs warning that a plank was about to fail.

We were examining the last of the hulls when he paused and shook his head. He beckoned me closer and indicated where the seams were bare. "Ran's fury has taken its toll - this one will need to be caulked", he said, and issued a sigh. "We have enough sheep wool and horse hair, but the last of the pine tar we used up at the beginning of the season."

"I will go into the forest and make a firepit to draw the tar from the wood", I suggested.

The erilar nodded. "While you toil in the hills", he said, "we will float the longboats and pack the hulls with salted fish, smoked joints of beef and barrels of water. I will make sure that the oars are oiled and that Atakam makes offerings to appease the gods of the wind and the water."

Early the following morning, I took Haldr and his men into the hills to remedy the situation. Ten of them spent the day felling half a dozen pine trees. Afterwards they chopped the fatwood into pieces as long as a man's leg and as thick as a forearm. Using a natural incline, the rest of us dug a pit which we lined with green birch bark. On the second day, we stacked the wood inside the earth pit and covered it with brushwood, green branches and turf before we set it alight.

It took most of the remainder of the day and the night for the red-black tar to trickle along the hollowed-out log at the bottom of the pit and fill the cauldron with black gold.

Come morning, I heaved the treasure onto my shoulder and made sure to leave an empty vessel underneath the log to catch the last of the tar that dripped from the firepit.

We went directly to the beach where Abdarakos was waiting with his men. I stripped down to my *braccae*, and for the rest of the day we wielded not axes, but caulking irons, methodically hammering the wool, hair and pitch into the seams between the planks.

The sun was low in the sky when Abdarakos spoke with me. "We have used up all the pine tar", he said. "And there are still seams that need caulking."

"When we left this morning, the smouldering fire was still drawing the last tar from the fatwood", I said. "There will be enough in the cauldron by now to fill the last seams."

"I will get the men to build pyres. We will finish this tonight, by the light of the flames", he said and gestured to the western horizon that had turned crimson. "Tomorrow there will be a storm. If the seams get water, we will be caulking a coffin-ship that will draw us down to the murky deeps."

I pulled my tunic over my tar-tangled hair and jogged up the hillside. But I had underestimated the effects of the last days' toil and I was forced to slow down to a walk after two miles at a run. By the time I reached the tar pit it was nearly dark, but light enough for me to notice that the vessel was nearly half-full with tar.

I sealed the cauldron, lifted it onto a shoulder, and turned around to pick my way down the hillside… and came face to face with an apparition that had appeared from nowhere. I staggered backwards and fell onto my backside, nearly dropping the cask of tar.

Kauko extended his arm.

I accepted and he pulled me to my feet.

The wild man pointed at the hills. "Many warriors moving through the forest", he said.

I shrugged. "It must be the Svear king and his young warriors", I replied. "We are expecting them on the morrow."

The hunter regarded me with his corpse-pale eyes, which seemed to shine silver in the moonlight. "Kauko knows when men are on their way to wet their blades. Tonight, the Earth Mother's thirst will be sated by blood", he said, his strange guttural accent chilling me to the bone.

With a sigh I heaved the vessel onto the ground, having made my decision. "Come", I said, and made my way down the hillside at a run. Although I heard not so much as a cracking twig or a single footfall, I knew that Kauko was never more than two paces behind.

* * *

A frown creased Abdarakos's brow when he noticed that I had returned empty-handed.

"There are men moving through the forest", I said.

"Did you lay eyes on them?" he growled, still clearly irritated.

"Come to my hall, war leader", I said. "And you will see."

My grandsire must have heard the iron in my voice. He issued a grunt and gestured for me to lead the way.

Five hundred heartbeats later, Atakam and Sigizan answered the erilar's summons and walked through the door of my hall. Runa hobbled closer and leaned on her linden stick, ready to give us Kauko's words to ensure that there was no misunderstanding.

Slowly and methodically Abdarakos questioned the pale man. With every answer that Runa translated, the war leader's countenance became darker until he eventually held up an open palm and turned to face the old seer.

"Tell the villagers to take what they can carry", he told Runa. "The ones who are not on board within a watch will be left behind. Tell them what is coming. Make sure they know they will be death-doomed if they stay."

Then he turned to Sigizan and Atakam. "All the warriors are to assemble on the beach, their sea-chests and their treasures loaded, and the oars at the ready."

"I will bring Kursik and Boarex from the warrior hall", my grandsire growled. "Ready the horses, Ragnar. I will meet you and Kauko at the gate."

Chapter 6 – Svear

Kauko ran with a tireless stride reminiscent of a wolf. Therefore, it was no surprise that when every so often he stopped, he sniffed the air like an animal would, and listened, cocking his head this way and that. For five miles we followed him along narrow moonlit tracks that for the most part did not allow two men to ride abreast.

Eventually he came to a halt and indicated for us to dismount.

"Leave horses", he said, and we followed on foot.

To our right, from across a deep ravine, we heard the sounds of men making their way through the woods.

The wolfman gestured for us to crouch down, and then he melted into the night.

On the other side of the gorge, less than thirty paces away, many dark shapes, who used their spears as walking sticks, passed by. We soon realised that Kauko had guided us to the flank of an army that was creeping towards our village.

Just then the hunter returned, carrying a trophy in each hand. He dropped it at my feet and retreated a step, the way I had seen pheasant hounds do when retrieving fowl for their master. "Seven, maybe eight times a hundred", he said.

Abdarakos lifted one of the severed heads and studied the features. "Svear", he said, and cast the blood-slick skull to the side. The erilar reached out and picked up the other head. He pointed to where the tail of a black fox was braided into the long black hair. "Suehan", he said. "They live to the north of the Svear. Their fox pelts are famous, even in the lands of Rome."

The erilar leaned in and lowered his voice. "King Othere does not like the Heruli telling him what he can and cannot do", he growled. "He has gathered his men and paid the Suehan in gold to march with him under the ruse that he is bringing young warriors to Runaville. Even now that we know that they are coming, we will not be able to stand against a force that outnumbers us more than ten to one."

"They will fall upon the village before we get our people onto the boats", Abdarakos continued. "We must attempt to distract them, to slow them down."

I waved Kauko closer. "Can we reach the tar pit before the Svear do?" I asked him.

The hunter turned his head to stare into the darkness, no doubt working out the route in his mind. "Try keep up", he said once we were mounted, and jogged off the way we had come. The erilar and I followed at a canter.

Arriving at the tar pit, I found the half-full cauldron where I had left it.

I ran to the fire pit and lifted a section of turf, exposing the smouldering wood to the air. Immediately flames leapt up from underneath, and I placed the cauldron on the fire. While the pitch heated up, I used the blunt end of my axe like a plough to cut a long, thin channel across the leaf-strewn soil.

When the tar was like honey, Abdarakos hefted the cauldron and poured the still warm pitch into the furrow. The remainder of the black liquid I smeared against the trunks of pines abutting the shallow trench.

No sooner had we finished our toil when we heard the noise of approaching men.

When the warriors of the Svear were but fifty paces away, I dropped glowing embers onto the molten tar. Within moments, a fifty-pace-wide wall of fire rose from the earth. The flames engulfed the trees I had blackened with pitch, and soon the woods turned into a raging inferno of smoke and fire, blocking the advance of Othere's army.

* * *

It must have been close to the middle hour of the night when the last of the villagers found themselves crowded onto the decks of the longboats.

Kursik arrived at the beach and handed the reins of his lathered mount to the men who were loading the animals. "They are close, erilar", he said.

Abdarakos took a flaming torch into his fist and he and I led a handful of his ringmen along the winding path up to the fortified village. When we had gone through the gate, he barked instructions to his men and walked with me to my hall.

"Do it", he growled.

I spun the torch onto the thatch. It felt like burying a dagger in my own chest. For a span of heartbeats there was only smoke, but then the first yellow tongues appeared. Soon the whole of the roof was aflame and clumps of burning reed dropped through the lattice onto the bone-dry wood, lighting up the structure I had toiled to build. More than that, it felt like I was burning the memories of my time with Unni and Runa – of my time with the Svear. But there was something else as well. Deep inside I felt the first flames of anger well up, sparked by hatred for the man who had caused it.

Abdarakos placed an arm around my shoulders. "When a warrior has to put his own hall to the torch, the fire of revenge keeps on burning for long", he said.

"How do you know, grandfather?" I asked.

"Because I have had to do it more than once myself", he said, and steered me back towards the gate of the flame-engulfed fort.

* * *

Not long after, I stood on the oak deck of Abdarakos's favourite ship, my arm wrapped around Unni's shoulders.

Hundreds of Svearmen streamed onto the beach where flames were consuming the ship we would never finish caulking. Amongst the warriors was a noble on a horse, none other than Othere himself.

Kursik reached for his quiver and put a shaft to the string, no doubt wanting to skewer the Svear king with an arrow.

Abdarakos reached out and pushed the bow down. "Do not deny Ragnar his vengeance", he growled. "My grandson will want to smell the Svear king's foul breath and see the fear in his eyes before his plunges his iron into Othere's black heart."

The erilar turned around without another word to make his way to the steering oar at the prow.

"I am sorry that you had to hear that, Unni", I said. "My grandfather is a warrior. He knows only the way of bloodshed and revenge."

Unni put her arms around my neck and pulled my face down to hers so that our lips nearly touched. "Ragnar, my love", she said. "Today you had to burn our home because of an evil king's lust for power. He has to pay. If you do not kill him, I will rip out his heart with my own hands and feed it to the dogs."

And then she kissed me.

* * *

Our longship glided south, across the moonlit blackness. Like ducklings paddling behind their mother, the other eight boats followed in our wake.

"Will Othere pursue us?" I asked my grandsire when a pinprick of light on the horizon was all that remained of the burning longship.

"I do not think that he will", the erilar growled, "but I also did not believe that he would attack us." He gestured at the women, children and animals crowding the deck. "Our ships are heavy and low in the water. We will row throughout the night while we are in familiar waters. Only when the sun sets tomorrow evening will we beach the hulls. The only thing that stands between these people and death is how well we pull the oars."

My turn to row soon arrived.

Kursik shifted to one side of his sea-chest to make room. I moved in beside him, placed my hands on the thick oak, and felt the rhythm of the stroke. When my sinews were warmed up, I nodded to the Hun, who relinquished the oar. Weaving through the press of humanity, he made his way to the stern where Unni scooped ale from an open vat. She handed him a horn and a piece of salted cod before he slumped down onto the deck.

Hours later, when the sun was low in the sky, Abdarakos leaned on the steering oar and the prow of the ship turned towards a distant beach. I silently thanked the gods. Every sinew in my back, legs and arms burned like fire. It was only my warrior pride that stopped me from begging Kursik to take over my shift.

One by one the other longships slid onto the shingle. While the men of the village butchered the sheep, goats and chickens that the erilar had selected, Sigizan and I rode out into the hinterland to ensure that we had not inadvertently landed close to a Gautar stronghold. Apart from a hastily vacated farm, we found no evidence of the presence of people, never mind warriors.

But Abdarakos was a wily old fox and he set a watch in the hills nonetheless. The gods favoured me and I drew the first shift. My hour passed without incident, and afterwards I joined Unni around the fire. I filled my belly with goat meat and fell asleep while trying to empty my second horn, the golden ale spilling onto the furs as I slumped down.

The erilar allowed us to sleep until the first rays appeared above the grey water.

Rather than waste time to break our fast on land, we hauled the longships into the water. While half of the warriors pulled at the oars, the others sated their hunger on the leftovers of the previous evening until it was their time to row.

This became our routine over the following twelve days. We rowed from sunrise to sunset, always keeping the coast within sight. From time to time we crossed paths with other longships, but none was foolish enough to approach.

The Gautar, who controlled the lands we passed, were no doubt aware of our presence. I am sure that they dispatched ships to hunt us, but our passage was too swift.

On the afternoon of the thirteenth day at sea, the coast fell away to the north, indicating that we were about to pass the southern tip of the Island of Scandza.

Abdarakos leaned on the steering oar and turned the prow-beast towards the shore. "It is twenty miles across open water to the land of the Danes", he said. "Tomorrow we will leave this shore at the time of the wolf and reach Daneland before the middle hour of the day. Once there, we will turn our hulls south and follow the coast."

"But we will have to be careful", the erilar added. "The Danes are better boatmen than the Gautar, and no friends of the Heruli."

Chapter 7 – White wind

We rowed in armour, our helmets within reach and our shields wedged between our sea chests and the board of the longboat.

A southwesterly breeze arrived with the rising sun. Ten heartbeats later, I felt a slight shudder as Abdarakos adjusted the steering oar to compensate for the force of the wind pushing us north. I noticed the erilar steal a glance at Atakam, whose gaze was fixed on the southern horizon.

When I had finished my shift, I relinquished the oar to Kursik and made my way to the stern. "It is the white wind", Abdarakos growled as I took the steering oar from him. "Pray to Ulgin that we reach the shores of Daneland before it turns into a ship-wrecker."

I noticed that the shaman did not offer his opinion, but was still staring into the distance.

Before I could enquire as to the reason, Atakam croaked, "Danes", and pointed somewhere to the west and south.

My grandsire took the oar from my fist and I vaulted onto the board of the ship, steadying myself with a hand on his shoulder. "Thirteen longships", I said. "All are under full oar."

Abdarakos studied the approaching Sea Danes for a span of heartbeats.

"We cannot outrow them", he growled, "because our hulls are heavy with the people of the village. Even if we reach the distant shore before the Danes do, they will slaughter us on the beach."

He leaned on the oar and the longship veered to the south, into the wind. "No man is able to escape his fate", he said. "Let us attack the Dane scum to make sure that we are given the seats of honour when we arrive at the great mead hall of the gods."

Sigizan pressed the ram's horn to his lips and issued a series of notes. With practised skill, the steersmen at the oars of our other ships altered course. In less than two hundred heartbeats we managed to transform our formation into a straight battle line of nine longships bearing down on the enemy.

Without the necessity for an order, the Huns on each ship gave up their oars to comrades. Moments later, four bowmen crouched down behind every prow beast, their arrows already in their draw hands.

Without warning, the wind picked up and the open maw of the wooden beast of our ship issued an unearthly wail, like a *draugr* screaming for blood.

"Now", Sigizan said, and as one we pulled the strings to our ears. Nearly forty shafts arced down onto the enemy boats. The Danes may have been scum, but fools they were not - our arrows rained down into the wood of their raised shields. Three more times we aimed our shafts high into the grey sky until only a hundred paces separated us.

Boarex and I launched another high volley, but Sigizan and Kursik, who were the best of the best, released heavy, armour-piercing arrows at an almost flat trajectory, catching the shield-bearers who protected the helmsmen off-guard. The tamarisk shafts slammed into the bodies of Dane steersmen, and two ships in the centre of the enemy line veered from their course. Others reached for the oars and took the place of the doomed men, but two more arrows left the hemp and sinew strings. The shafts struck with the power of war hammers and spun the unfortunates overboard to leave the oars unattended.

Without a guiding hand on the steering oars, the ships swerved into the path of the other enemy boats. I heard the crack of wood as the oars splintered, and moments later the hulls slammed together. Four of the Danes' vessels floundered, removing them from the fight.

On Abdarakos's command, every second rower on our boat shipped his oar, donned a helmet, and gripped a shield.

Twenty heartbeats later, the enemy ships were upon us.

A large *skeid*, which must have sported at least twenty-five oars a side, headed straight at us, no doubt intending to manoeuvre alongside. I ducked behind the ship's board, and a moment later a spear whooshed overhead, missing me by inches. Less than a heartbeat later, the Dane tumbled over the board of their ship, clawing at Kursik's arrow that was lodged in his throat.

I ducked again to avoid another spear, and released a shaft at a helmetless Dane whirling a grappling iron. The broad-headed tip ripped open his skull and, entangled in the rope and chain, the iron dragged the corpse into the depths.

When the Dane ship was less than two oar lengths away, the brave, or mayhap the foolish amongst their numbers, hefted their weapons, raised their shields, and crouched down on the wooden rail above the board, ready to jump onto our deck.

I drew my bearded axe from its sheath on my back and held the weapon at the ready in a middle-guard.

Again, the wind gained strength, howling through the oarlocks.

Five paces separated us from the chanting enemy, when a Dane launched himself at me from atop the railing of the approaching ship.

Not only was I as strong as a bear, but I had trained with the bearded axe since boyhood. My right hand slid down the ash haft and the blunt end of the iron head moved through the air like lightning, striking the warrior's shield dead centre on the round copper boss. The impact must have shattered his left arm, and with a scream of agony he fell short, slamming into the board. In desperation he dropped his sword and reached out with his good hand to grip the railing.

I raised my axe to sever his arm, but the wind drove the ships together and the warrior was crushed between the clinker hulls like a louse squashed between fingernails.

"Beware", Kursik shouted.

Frantically my eyes darted this way and that, believing that I had failed to notice an attack.

"Down", Kursik boomed.

I trusted the Hun with my life, so I slumped down onto my backside.

A wall of water hit me from behind, hurling me against the board of the ship. All around I heard screams as men, women and horses were being washed overboard.

The wind and waves rocked the ships violently, the riveted timber creaking under immense strain.

I realised that the ocean's assault had made me forget about the enemy, but I noticed that, like us, the Danes were suddenly more interested in saving themselves than attacking us.

"Sever the chains", Abdarakos boomed, to be heard above the roar of the waves and the howling of the wind. "The ship-wrecker has come. Tonight I do not want to sleep in the bed of Ran."

Two paces to my right I noticed a chain-backed grappling hook embedded in the oak. The iron was used to ensure that the binding could not be severed, but the blade of my axe was crafted from the finest steel and it not only cut the links, but also bit deep into the railing underneath. With the rope severed, the force of the violent waves tore the hulls away from each other and I lost my balance. I tumbled overboard, but managed to retain my grip on the axe.

I breathed a sigh of relief and started to heave myself onto the ship, but then the two hulls that were still attached at their sterns, came smashing back. I realised that I would not gain the deck in time, but a corpse-pale head appeared, and two fur-bound arms grasped my armour and yanked me back to safety.

The hulls crashed together with such force that the last remaining grapple broke free from the oak railing, and I heard the sound of iron rivets being ripped from planking.

"To the oars! To the oars!" Abdarakos yelled. The deck heaved underneath my feet and I fell heavily, rolled over, and amidst the chaos managed to get my oar through the lock and into the foaming sea. I started booming the timing of the stroke, but there were not enough oars in the water, causing the ship to spin around aimlessly. I kept at it until Beremud plonked onto his sea chest and added his oar. Thirty heartbeats later we had twenty oars in the water. I felt the longship turn. Again, we heaved and nearly tipped over, but the gods chose not to claim the ship. We settled into the stroke, and with the wind at our stern, we sped across the roaring ocean with the speed of a galloping horse.

The water rose around my feet, and I called out for assistance. Unni, who crouched beside Runa near the centre of the deck, answered my call.

Soon the villagers were dumping buckets of saltwater over the board in an effort to keep us afloat. But no mortal can fight the sea and win. Slowly but surely the water rose, albeit at a slower rate.

Many of the warriors had taken wounds, and the men pulling at the oars knew that there would be no relief until our hull slid onto the shingle, or Ran enfolded us in her chilling embrace. For two hours I fought the waves until I could not get my sinews to respond. Others, who had toiled at the oars, had already yielded to fatigue. I lifted the wooden blade from the water and slumped forward onto the shaft.

The bony fingers of a skeletal hand clasped the base of my neck and thin, icy lips pressed against my ear. "Do it for the child, Iron One", Runa screeched, to be heard above the noise of the storm.

I looked into her rheumy eyes and I knew that she had communed with the gods. Somehow Ulgin gave me strength. I dipped my oar back into the ocean and pulled the shaft for one more stroke. And then another... and another.

Two hours later, our waterlogged hull scraped over the shingle. I tried to rise, but fell over onto the rough-hewn timber and willingly surrendered to the blackness.

Chapter 8 – Hrothgar

I came to when Unni pressed the rim of a wooden bowl against my chapped lips.

"Drink", she said, and I obeyed, slurping greedily at the thick, salty broth.

When I tried to rise, she firmly pushed me back onto the furs. "Give the pottage time to strengthen your body", she said. "You are the only one who rowed all the way to the beach. I have heard the other warriors say that your sinews are forged of iron."

"How long did I sleep?" I asked.

"A full cycle of the sun", she said.

"And the other ships?" I asked.

"Five hulls are drawn up on the beach over yonder", she said. "Of the others, only driftwood and bloated corpses remain."

I suddenly remembered Runa's words. "Are you with child?" I asked.

A frown furrowed Unni's brow. "No", she replied. "Why do you ask?"

Just then Runa shuffled in underneath the canvas canopy. "The villagers need your guidance, child", she said to her granddaughter. "I will look after him."

Unni nodded, stood, and disappeared.

"You told me Unni was with child", I accused Runa.

"Did I?" she said. "Or did you dream it?"

I narrowed my eyes.

"You and Unni are both alive", she said, waving her hand dismissively. "Do not concern yourself with the machinations of the gods, Ragnar." Then a hint of a smile played along the corners of her mouth, "Soon, other things will occupy your mind, warrior."

The old seer had hardly uttered the words when I heard a commotion in our camp. Moments later Abdarakos and Sigizan arrived.

"Ragnar has found his way back to the world of man, erilar", Runa announced.

My grandsire acknowledged her words with a grunt.

"Come, Ragnar", he said. "Your rest is done. Kursik has returned from scouting the lay of the land. A warband of Spear Danes are on their way."

* * *

I followed Abdarakos and Sigizan to their tent where Kursik was waiting. The Hun's lathered horse was tethered nearby, and it was clear that he had pushed the weary animal close to its limits.

Kursik acknowledged me with a nod. "The Dane warband is but twelve miles away. A mounted lord leads three hundred spearmen. His ringmen, maybe fifty or so, have good armour with swords strapped to their belts, but the rest…", he shrugged to indicate his obvious doubt in the Danes' abilities.

"There are too many", Abdarakos said. "Only one hundred and twenty of our warriors still draw breath, and half of them carry wounds that will take weeks to heal. Sixty cannot stand against three hundred."

"The ships?" I asked.

Sigizan shook his head. "All have sprung planks. The best we can do is makeshift repairs", he said, and gestured to the choppy sea, "but the waves will soon tear holes in the hulls."

"The Danes are advancing from the southwest", Sigizan said. "We cannot flee because our path to the north is blocked by moors."

The Hun raised an open palm before I could ask the obvious question. "I have tried to enter the fens", he said, and turned his head away in resignation. "But only a wolf will be able to find its way across the bog. Any man who dares to cross will be death-doomed for sure."

I turned to leave.

"Where are you going?" Abdarakos asked.

"I will speak with a wolf and return", I said, and went off in search of Kauko.

* * *

Kauko stared at the water-logged ground. "What you want, Iron One?" he asked.

"A hiding place for all of us", I replied.

The wolfman issued a nod and disappeared amongst the trees rising from the waterlogged soil.

Close to an hour later, Kauko emerged from the bog-woods. He nodded absentmindedly as he strolled past.

"Did you find a place where we can hide from the Danes?" I asked.

"Yes", he replied, and carried on making his way towards the camp.

* * *

It took nearly two hours for Kauko to lead the survivors of the shipwreck safely through the bog forest. Every so often, a warrior, villager or animal would stray off the path that the hunter had marked with sticks. Most times, it required many hands to free them from the stinking black mud that greedily tried to pull them into the murky depths.

Eventually we emerged onto a grassy expanse of higher, dry ground.

Abdarakos gestured to the surrounding swamp. "These bogs are better than stone walls", he declared, and stole a glance at Kauko. "No man will dare follow us."

"Come, Ragnar", he added. "Let us put my words to the test."

While the women and villagers busied themselves with setting up camp, Abdarakos led the bowmen amongst the warriors along the stake-marked path to the edge of the swamp. We carefully removed the markers at the edge of the swamp and retreated a hundred paces into the wetland, making sure that we would be noticed by an approaching enemy.

We did not have to wait long for the warband of Spear Danes to arrive – no doubt having followed our trail. They paused at the edge of the bogwood where our tracks disappeared into the swamp. Judging by the animated discussion between the lord and his oathsworn, it was clear that they found it hard to believe that we had entered the fens.

"Kill one of the lord's ringmen", Abdarakos said.

Five heartbeats later, Sigizan's arrow slammed into the chest of a warrior, who stumbled backwards clutching at the shaft.

Still they did not advance.

The erilar nodded, and two more arrows left Sigizan's horn and sinew bow in quick succession. Two more men fell. Then Abdarakos stepped out from the mogshade and shouted a challenge to the noble.

The Dane lord pointed his spear at my grandsire, and in response his warriors surged forward into the mire.

"Now we wait", Abdarakos said, leaning on his spear.

A hundred heartbeats later, the swamp was dotted with stricken men trapped by the putrid black mud. The warriors who somehow managed to remain on solid ground went to the aid of their comrades, only to fall prey to the bog themselves.

In their struggle to escape from the mud pits they abandoned their shields and spears. One by one the Huns picked off their prey with well-aimed arrows. When the fifty Dane warriors had perished in the mud, the erilar gestured for us to follow him. "Come, let us return to our people", he said and, with a sucking sound, plucked the first of the remaining stakes from the mud.

* * *

When the sun had set, Abdarakos and Atakam came to the tent I shared with Unni and Runa to join us beside the cooking fire.

"We are stranded on this foreign shore", my grandsire said. "The Dane lord would have laid claim to our longships."

"This lord is not a Sea Dane", Runa croaked. "The ships that attacked us come from the lands of the south. He would have put them to the torch or traded the hulls to his kin, the Sea Danes, for coin."

"Under whose dominion is this land?" I asked.

"These shores are ruled by a lord of the Spear Danes who believes himself a king", Runa said. "Hrothgar won much fame in battle over the years, but time has caught up with him", she added, and I could not help but notice that her gaze remained on the erilar.

"We must attempt to reach my sword brother Mourdagos, the war leader of the Boat Heruli", my grandsire said. "He will give us refuge. Then we will gather warriors under our banner so that we may reclaim that which Othere has stolen."

"Yet we cannot reach Mourdagos without longships", Atakam remarked. "The gods have brought us to this place for a reason."

"What is the reason?" Abdarakos asked, clearly irritated at the shaman's words. "And when will they reveal our fate?"

"Do not try to dictate time and place to the heavens, warrior", Atakam growled, chastising the erilar. "The gods play by their own rules and have no regard for the whims of man."

Abdarakos did not take kindly to the scolding and fixed Atakam with a glare from his good eye.

"We have only enough food to last for three, maybe four days", Unni said softly. "We lost most of our provisions in the storm."

"Mayhap the gods have brought us here to do what we do best", I remarked, and took a swallow of ale.

"And what is that?" Atakam asked.

"Redden our blades with the blood of our enemies and claim the spoils of war", I said. "Tomorrow, Kauko, Kursik and I will scout the lair of the Danes, then, Atakam, if the gods and the war leader wills it, we should go there and have our revenge on Hrothgar."

Suddenly the words of the shaman were forgotten. My grandsire grinned proudly, raised his ale horn, and emptied it with one long swallow.

Chapter 9 – Mead hall

Keeping to the shadows, I pointed at the imposing oak building a hundred paces distant. Hrothgar's great mead hall, flanked by two smaller longhouses, had been built against the slope of a hill, affording the lord a view across the sprawling village located on the flat ground below. Enormous beech posts topped with oak beams served as the foundation. Wide wooden steps led up to double doors carved in the likeness of a stag – the symbol of royalty.

"They believe that they are untouchable", Kursik said, referring to the glaring absence of a defensive wall.

"The hall itself looks to be as strong as a fort", I replied.

Kursik used his chin to indicate thralls who were carrying vats of ale and ripened boar carcasses into the hall through a servant's door at the side of the building. "They are preparing for a feast", he said, "and by the looks of it, it will be this night."

* * *

"Hrothgar is a powerful lord", Abdarakos said once Kursik and I had finished our tale. "It would be foolish to underestimate him. If we keep poking the bear, he will eventually come to the fens to have his revenge, no matter what the cost."

"Only fear will keep him at bay", Atakam said.

"Hrothgar is a warrior", Sigizan said. "He does not fear us because his warriors outnumber ours four to one."

"If he can be convinced that we are not men, but something else ..., something darker, he will not dare lead his warriors into the misty moors. Hrothgar will remain in his hall and tremble at the mention of our name."

"Others Danes, his kin, will come to his aid", Abdarakos said. "Maybe even his Gautar allies."

"They will", Atakam agreed. "And some will have boats", he added, a sly smile curving his thin lips.

* * *

Concealed by the darkness, I crept closer until the Dane was but a step away. I reached out and clamped my hand over the mouth of the warrior, pulled back his head, and slid the iron of my dagger across his throat. When the corpse became limp, I gently laid it down on the damp soil.

Once Kursik, Beremud and Kauko had dealt with the other sentries, they fell in behind me. All of us were wrapped in furs, with our faces, hair and hands blackened with soot. Few would believe that we were men because in the darkness we seemed like walking wolves, fearsome apparitions that had pried open the door bolt of the Black Gates.

"Do you have it?" I asked Beremud in a low whisper.

He issued a grunt of confirmation and gestured to a pouch slung across his shoulders. The big Goth crouched down, removed two severed bear paws from the satchel, and wetted them with the blood of the dead men.

I nodded and started up the moonlit path towards the side door, which I assumed gave access to an area where thralls could toil and sweat to prepare food without giving offence to their masters. We waited for our eyes to become accustomed to the dim light provided by the dying embers of the cooking fire. Vats of ale and mead, smoked joints of pork and beef, pots of honey, and large rounds of cheese adorned the rough timber shelves lining the walls.

With great care we brought the provisions outside and gestured for Sigizan, who was accompanied by a dozen of the erilar's oathsworn, to approach. The warriors heaved the vats onto their shoulders, deposited the joints and cheeses into canvas pouches, and silently disappeared down the path. Others, I knew would be hauling sacks of wheat and barley from the grain stores of the Danes.

The great stag hall of the lord of the land was bathed in a dull orange hue still emanating from what remained of the thick oak and beech logs smouldering in the hearth. Inside, the smoke-filled room was thick with the aroma of roasted boar and barley ale. I had to remind myself that we had not come to feast, but to sow the seeds of fear.

Once Beremud had stained the floor with bloody bear paw prints, he joined Sigizan outside. Kursik, Kauko and I made our way to the centre of the hall. All around us, snoring, fur-covered shapes were sprawled on the floor or draped over benches. Once near the hearth, we hefted heavy wooden clubs onto which we had strapped the paws of a bear.

I drew a deep breath and issued a feral roar that echoed off the walls.

Within less than a heartbeat the hall became a milling mass of confused warriors. Kursik, Kauko and I made our way towards the side door, viciously clearing our path with the bear-paw clubs. Warriors screamed and roared as they ran each other through with their blades, not knowing friend from foe.

When we entered the treeline, the violent clash of blades from inside the hall of Hrothgar could still be heard.

* * *

The food and ale we looted from the Danes were enough to sustain us for weeks, but we all knew that it would not last through the winter.

On a chilly afternoon, a week after the raid, Boarex sent for me.

The Huns managed to catch an unfortunate peasant who had ventured too close to the moors, a poacher who had set his traps for squirrels and hares where the king would be less likely to notice.

I was met by the sight of Kursik leaning against a beech, nonchalantly running a whetstone along the iron of his dagger.

Two paces away, a man sat on the ground, wearing a resigned expression. A rope was tied around his scrawny neck, with the other end secured to the Hun's saddle. As is almost always the case with peasants, he was of an indeterminable age.

"How old are you? I asked in the tongue of the Svear, emphasising every word so that he would understand.

"Next year I will be thirty seasons old, lord", the man replied, and offered me a gap-toothed smile.

Trokondas had taught me a thing or two about dealing with his kind.

I drew my blade and took a step closer.

The smile disappeared from the poacher's face.

"What is the gossip amongst Hrothgar's oathsworn?" I asked, making sure to rhythmically move the tip of my blade to give clarity to the man's thoughts.

"They say that an ancient evil has made its home in the fens, lord", the man replied. "It was this evil creature that, but a week ago, attacked the warriors in the stag hall of the king, they say."

I gestured for him to continue.

"The beast must have come from the darkness below", he said. "It killed thirty of the king's ringmen without taking a wound. The thralls who washed the blood from the timber said that the tracks were not left by men. Some ringmen still nurse terrible wounds where the thing's claws had ripped open their flesh. One liegeman saw it all. He swore on his blade that it was a skin-changer who transformed from a man into a bear."

The poacher flicked his tongue, licking the spittle from his moist lips.

"Since then, I bar the inside of my door at night, lord", he said.

"Have you told all?" I asked and moved another step closer.

The peasant tried to retreat, but was jerked back when the rope around his neck tightened.

"King Hrothgar has sent word to his allies across the Eastern Sea, the thralls say. He has called for a great champion to help him rid the land of evil."

"Champion?" I asked.

The man nodded vigorously. "A warrior of much reputation, lord", he said.

"What is his name?" I asked.

"Slaughter-wolf is what they call him, lord", the peasant replied, and again his tongue flicked out of his maw.

Chapter 10 – Champion

I waved Kauko closer, imparted my instructions in a whisper, and the wild man melted into the greenwood. Then I sheathed my blade and turned away from the poacher.

"I will do it", Kursik volunteered with relish, and slipped his dagger from its scabbard.

I harboured no doubts about what the Hun's intentions were. "No", I said and turned back to the peasant.

"You will not tell your lord of our encounter", I commanded, my hand still on the hilt of my sword.

"I swear it on the life of my children, lord", the man pleaded. "I will not go to Lord Hrothgar's hall." He shook his head vigorously as if to convince himself, muttering, "No, lord, never, lord."

"I grant you your life", I said, and flicked the wretch a silver.

Kursik bore witness to my clemency with pursed lips, but still cut away the rope at my gesture. "He will run to his lord and tell all", the Hun said. "Do you never learn, Son of Attila?"

"We will see", I muttered as the peasant scurried off into the undergrowth like a frightened animal released from a trap.

"Come, we must go tell the erilar", I said. "He needs to know that Hrothgar has called on the Gautar for help."

* * *

"I have heard the name of Slaughter-wolf", Abdarakos said, and took a draught of ale. "Hygelac, the Gautar king, is his uncle. The young warrior has won much fame in the Gautar wars against the savage tribes of the North. They say that one day he will sit in the seat of power."

"The prince will be accompanied by his ringmen", Atakam said. "He will arrive with much fanfare and many ships."

Abdarakos nodded his agreement. "I will post a sentry near the beach so that we are forewarned."

Just then a guard pushed open the flap of the erilar's tent. "Lord", he said, "the wolfman wants to speak with Ragnar."

Abdarakos grunted his consent and Kauko was ushered into our presence. I noticed that he clasped something in his fist, which, moments later, he presented to me on the open palm of an outstretched hand.

It proved to be a human ear with a large flap of skin still attached. Undoubtedly the appendage was crudely cut from a corpse. Beside the ear was a blood-stained coin - the silver I had earlier given to the poacher.

"Peasant tried to go to king's mead hall", Kauko said, and by way of explanation, tapped a hand against his sheathed obsidian dagger.

"Did you tell Kursik?" I asked, because I did not want the Hun to gloat.

"No", he said, closed his fist around the gory trophy, turned around, and left.

"What was that about?" my grandsire asked with a raised eyebrow.

"I am too trusting", I replied.

"A man has to know his weaknesses", Abdarakos said, and slapped my back in a gesture of approval.

* * *

"I heard that earlier, Kauko strolled around camp with an ear in his hand", Kursik said that evening when we were seated around my hearth.

"They are a base and savage lot", I said, referring to the tribe of hunters that the wild man belonged to.

With a wink, the Hun passed me the coin that Kauko had retrieved from the peasant's corpse. "You may be trusting, but you are no fool, Son of Attila", Kursik said.

"Thank you", I replied, rubbed the worst of the gore from the silver, and dropped it into my purse.

Just then Runa shuffled into the tent and joined Unni, Kursik and me around the fire. She slowly lowered herself onto the furs and handed a leather satchel to the Hun. "Go, and give this to the war leader", she said.

Kursik half-heartedly nodded his agreement and chugged the ale remaining in his horn before he disappeared into the night.

I recognised the faraway look in Runa's eyes and knew that she had sent Kursik away for a reason. She had no doubt been somewhere in the woods communing with the gods and her words were only meant for Unni and me.

"When the ships come and the war-wolf of the Gautar draws his blade, careful you must be, Ragnar", she said. "He is a giant slayer, a god-touched ravager."

"You should avoid this man, Ragnar", Unni said. "He sounds dangerous."

"No!" the old seer screeched, chastising her granddaughter. "No, child, do not dare stand against the fate that the gods have ordained."

"Have you seen my death?" I asked Runa. "Will I die when I meet this warrior blade to blade?"

"Only the gods know when a man must cross the bridge", she said, suddenly dismissive. "Do I look like a god to you?"

Kursik ducked into the tent.

Runa gained her feet and returned whence she came, but her words left a lingering blackness - a dark shadow that lay heavily on my shade.

* * *

Late afternoon the following day, my grandsire summoned me.

"Four longships have been sighted off the mainland", Abdarakos said, and indicated a messenger standing near the flap. "Go with him, Ragnar, and see who arrives from across the Austmarr."

I accompanied the oathsworn warrior, weaving our way along the stake-marked path. Eventually we left the fens behind and made our way towards the water, keeping to the overgrown ravines.

Once we reached the seashore, the warrior led me to the cliffs overlooking the beach. We went down onto our hands and knees and crawled right up to where the exposed roots of a gnarled old beech desperately clung to the crumbling face in an effort to avoid toppling over the edge.

We spied four large warships gliding across the mirror surface of the water. One by one the timber hulls grated onto the shingle. As the lead *skeid* grinded to a halt, the warrior who had been holding onto the prow beast jumped down onto the gravel. Even though he wore full armour he landed with the grace of a predator, reminding me of the lions the emperor of the East kept for his pleasure.

"My sister's son sailed away to earn fame and fortune across the water, lord", the warrior lying beside me whispered. "Three years ago, he came home with armour not unlike that.

He gained it from a Saxon lord on the island the Romans call Britannia."

I took my time to study the hulking warrior.

The blackened steel plates of his riveted iron helmet accentuated the burnished brass crest, brow-guards, and nasal - all decorated with intricate etching. At the rear of the helm, an apron of thick chain protected a bull-like neck.

Around his powerful shoulders hung a thick-woven crimson wool cloak edged with fox fur. His torso was encased in a short-sleeved chainmail byrnie that extended to his knees. The iron had no doubt been scrubbed and oiled, and shone like silver in the rays of the sun.

Many gold and silver armbands were clamped around his bulging, veined upper arms. The brass-edged vambraces on his forearms were forged from black steel and matched the greaves strapped to his lower legs.

Suspended from a thick black leather belt were the hilts of a *seax* and shortsword. The pommels bore no jewels nor gold, but were workmanlike pieces of quality.

It was clear that the warrior was no stranger to war.

Close to where we lay, a partridge suddenly took flight - no doubt to flee a predator.

Slaughter-wolf's head jerked about like lightning, the cheek guards of his helmet screeching as he did. His gaze scanned the hinterland and settled on our hiding place. Then his right hand went to the hilt of his blade and slowly he drew the gleaming iron. I was convinced that the strange champion had sensed our presence.

But then a party of mounted Spear Danes appeared at the top of the well-used path that led down to the beach.

The warrior's oathsworn spilled from the deck of the longships and flanked their lord, who tore his gaze away from us and slipped his blade back into the sheath.

Slaughter-wolf turned to face the approaching riders.

The welcoming party reined in ten paces from the men on the shingle beach. To display his peaceful intent, the lead rider grounded the haft of his lance. "I am warden to king Hrothgar, who exerts dominion over these lands", the man boomed. "State your business in the land of the Spear Danes."

The hulking warrior strolled forward three paces.

The warden's horse, sensing that his rider had been caught off guard, retreated a step.

The warrior stopped. "I am Slaughter-wolf of the War-Geats", he growled, and his voice matched his intimidating appearance. "We are ringmen to Hygelac, the ruler of the lands across the Austmarr. Our king has sent us west to answer the call of Hrothgar whose lands are threatened by fen-dwelling creatures."

"The king is expecting you, lord", the warden said, and bowed his head. He issued a whispered instruction to an underling, and moments later the Gautar champion was presented with a mount.

Slaughter-wolf swung up onto the horse's back and I noticed that, although he sat comfortably in the saddle, riding was not his forte. "Fifty men must remain with the ships", he commanded a close companion.

"And I will arrange for the same number of King Hrothgar's warriors to aid your men who remain behind", the warden said. "One hundred men will be enough to ensure that your hulls are protected."

Then the Gautar warrior kicked his gelding to a trot and led the way up the path. Behind him followed a hundred of his ringmen.

Chapter 11 – Arm

The sun was still high in the sky when I returned to the Heruli camp in the moors.

"Ulgin, in his great wisdom, has given us a way out", Atakam said once I had told all. "But he wishes to test our iron against the warriors who guard the ships."

"They outnumber us, but if we fall upon them in the hours of darkness, we might prevail", Abdarakos said.

"It will take time to clear the beach of enemies and get the women, children and animals on board", Sigizan cautioned. "If the warriors of king Hrothgar and his Gautar allies are alerted to the fighting, they will come rushing to the seashore and fall upon our rear. Trapped between two forces, we will be slaughtered to a man."

"Then we must make sure that Hrothgar and the Gautar champion are otherwise occupied", I suggested.

The war leader nodded and gestured for me to elaborate.

* * *

As soon as the darkness was thick enough to conceal us, Kauko, Boarex and I arrived at the edge of the forest near the mead hall of the Dane king. Kursik and Beremud had wanted to join us, but Abdarakos needed to bolster his thinned-out ranks, especially with archers. Boarex was still nursing an injury to his draw arm, so the erilar reluctantly agreed for him to accompany us.

Close to the middle hour of the night, a light easterly breeze picked up. Soon a thin mist, that smelled of the sea, rolled down the hillside. Later, when the sounds of feasting and debauchery eventually ceased, the great stag hall of Hrothgar was shrouded in fog.

I nodded to the wolfman, who drew his stone blade and vanished into the shadows. Kauko returned a few hundred heartbeats later, the smell of blood clinging to him like a wet cloak to armour.

With the sentries eliminated, Boarex and I went crouching through the mist until we stood before the stag-carved oak. I pushed against the heavy timber, and silently the door of the great hall swung open.

Like the last time we had visited, the glowing embers revealed dark shapes where Gautar and Dane liegemen had succumbed to ale and mead. The only sound was the rhythmic snoring of men.

Boarex and I were halfway to the centre of the hall when a voice cut through the smell of sweat, ale and woodsmoke.

"I have waited long for your arrival, Herulian", a man growled in the tongue of the Gautar.

Judging by the clarity of the voice, it was obvious that whomever had spoken had not partaken in the debauchery.

The two of us came to an abrupt halt. Still, no one stirred and the snoring continued unabated.

Twenty heartbeats later, a dark hulking form rose from the far side of the hearth, accompanied by the familiar sound of scale and mail rubbing against a harness.

"Tonight, I will send you back through the Black Gates whence you came", the voice growled, thick with menace.

Boarex pulled me closer so that my forehead touched his, "I will fight him, Ragnar. You and the hunter must draw them into the swamps. The wild man heeds only your commands – he will abandon me if you fall."

I started to object, but my friend squeezed my arm and pushed past me to confront the approaching champion.

"Go!" Boarex shouted as he and the Gautar warrior came together.

The Hun's shout had the desired effect. All around us oathsworn warriors began to stir and reach for their blades and spear hafts.

The first of the Gautar ringmen came at me in an attempt to block my way to the door. I smashed my fist into where I believed his face was, and was rewarded with a wet crunching sound. Another tried to storm me from the side, but I stepped from his path and slammed my knee into his temple.

And then I was outside. Running, I glanced over my shoulder to see warriors spilling from the hall.

I stumbled along the path, then into the treeline, sure that I would be caught in moments, all the while cursing the foolishness of my plan. Then a skin-bound arm reached out from the side of the track and drew me into the undergrowth.

"Come, Iron One", Kauko said. "Go where I go."

I stole a final glance at the mead hall of the king. In that moment a terrible scream reached my ears, and I knew in my heart that it was Boarex.

For the best part of an hour, the hunter and I led the pursuing warriors in circles through the forest until we had drawn them into the moorlands. Then he gripped my forearm, and like a mother would a child, half-dragged me through the greenwood with a confidence that was hard to comprehend.

When we finally stumbled onto the beach, it was clear that the fight for possession of the boats had been over for a while. The shingle was littered with the arrow-riddled corpses of Gautar and Danes. Heruli oathsworn and Svear were frantically loading women, children and animals onto the captured longships that had already been pushed into the water.

To one side, another group of oathsworn were building a pyre for our warriors who had fallen in the battle.

I spied Abdarakos, Sigizan and Atakam on the deck of the largest warship where the erilar was shouting orders to his men. Close by I noticed Unni and Runa, both safely on board.

"You have done well, Ragnar", my grandsire boomed when I arrived at the water's edge. Then he noticed that Boarex was not at my side and his smile vanished.

"I ran away like a coward while Boarex stood alone against the Gautar champion", I said.

"If you had not led Hrothgar's men into the fens, we would all be corpses", Sigizan said. "Come aboard, Ragnar, the ships are nearly loaded."

"I will come when I am ready", I said, turned away, and walked to the edge of the cliffs where, eons ago, giant boulders had tumbled onto the shingle.

I climbed the highest rock and sat down cross-legged on the rough stone.

Reaching behind my back, I drew my axe from its sheath, and by the silver light of the waxing moon I carved Ulgin's sacred markings into the ash haft of my bearded blade. Slowly and deliberately, I pierced my own flesh with the iron of my dagger and cut the rune of vengeance into the palm of my left hand. With the bloodied hand I gripped my right wrist. Muttering the words I had learned on the lap of Atakam, I invoked the power of the *Alfars*, the ancient ones.

I sheathed my blade and strolled to where the last of the Heruli warriors were trudging through the water to board the longships. A dozen paces from the shoreline, the funeral pyre of our fallen was burning brightly. The yellow flame tongues reached to the heavens, sending the shades of our dead across the bridge of stars to the mead hall of the gods where they would be welcomed as heroes.

I said a prayer to Ulgin for the soul of Boarex, and waded into the water that was as cold and dark as the realm of Hella.

Beremud and Kursik had hardly hauled me onto the timber deck when I heard the chants of warriors who streamed down the cliff paths onto the shingle.

Abdarakos ordered our rowers to push the oars into the water.

The Gautar and Danes came to a halt five paces from the water's edge. In the front rank I spied a hulking form adorned in black and brass armour.

Slaughter-wolf handed his shield to his weapons bearer and waded two paces into the water, the gentle waves lapping at his greaves.

He drew his sword and pointed the gleaming blade straight at me. "There you are, coward", he roared. "Come and face me, or are you afraid that you will meet the same fate as your death-doomed brother."

From the ranks of Gautar a warrior cast a severed arm onto the shingle. Adorning the bloody appendage, I recognised the arm rings and the vambrace of my Hun friend. It appeared as if the arm had not been severed but rather ripped off by something or someone possessing immense strength. I should have been afraid then, but rather, a red-hot rage rose from deep inside.

I felt Abdarakos's hand tighten around my arm. "Ignore the fool, Ragnar", the erilar growled. "The Gautar champion is livid because you have outwitted him and taken his boats. Godlike strength and skill without cunning is useless. Boarex gave his life willingly. Tonight, he feasts with Ulgin and the great warriors of our people."

I issued a nod, but as I turned around to go to Unni, I stared into the face of Atakam. My eyes met his, and although there were no words, I knew what had to be done.

"Fight me, coward!" Slaughter-wolf roared again, his fists clenched and the veins bulging in his troll-like neck.

I took another step towards my wife, and the erilar relaxed his grip. Then I nodded to Unni and Runa, tore free from Abdarakos's hold, spun around, and dived head-first into the Austmarr.

Chapter 12 – Shingle

My feet found the gravel at the same time that my fist tightened around the haft of my bearded axe.

The Gautar did not rush me like a fool would, but waited patiently for me to come to him. On his lips he wore a smirk that spoke of supreme confidence, as if the gods had already shown him the outcome of the fight.

"Not only are you a coward", Herulian", he sneered in the tongue of the Svear, "but you are a fool."

"I have killed more pups like you than I care to remember", he spat. "You were no doubt sired by a warrior in some backwater – a self-styled chieftain. You honed your skills against the peasants of the village, and now, having bested serfs and thralls, you believe that you are a warrior of renown."

The sacred runes of vengeance burned against the palm of my right hand. It became hotter and hotter until it felt as if I were clasping a blade that been drawn from a blazing forge.

So occupied was I with the gods that I barely heard the blabbering of the Gautar, who must have interpreted my silence as acknowledgement that his speculation was grounded in fact. This, in turn, emboldened him to elaborate about his own achievements.

"I have fought in the lands across the great water, side by side with Hengist the Saxon lord. I have slain Romans, Britons, Picts – none could stand against me." He spat in the water to show his contempt. "Now you, a pup who has crawled from the mud of Svearland, think that you can best me."

Slowly the Gautar moved forward, trying to get close enough for his blade to strike a death blow.

I held my axe in a middle-guard, both hands on the haft - my left palm facing upward and the right down. To a man who had not been trained by the elite guards of the Eastern Empire it must have appeared clumsy, unwieldy.

Slaughter-wolf's sword flashed brightly, reflecting the flames consuming our fallen – a thrust powerful enough to punch through the hull of a ship – never mind my armour.

In response I moved my left foot back and to the side, allowing me to twist my body to avoid the path of the sword. But Slaughter-wolf was faster than I believed possible. Although his iron only brushed along my excubitor armour, it ripped the scales from the mailed backing.

The Gautar champion did not overreach. With the same adder-like speed he stepped back, his form near perfect and more than sufficient to avoid a counter strike. But the men who had trained me in the way of the axe knew no equal. I lunged forward with my right foot, following the retreating champion. My left hand relinquished its grip, but my right fist remained on the haft, close to the iron head. The brass-wrapped butt came around with speed and struck Slaughter-wolf on the side of his blackened helmet.

The blow was powerful enough to daze an ordinary warrior, but the Gautar shook off the strike with a shake of his head and a roll of his shoulders.

I did not hurt him in the least, but for less than a heartbeat he paused. His hesitation was almost imperceptible, but it showed me that I had sown the seeds of doubt.

"Even the serfs and peasants of my little village move better than you do, old man", I growled.

Using the haft as an extension of my left arm, I punched at his face. My left fist still clutched the ash right behind the axe head and I made sure to stay on the left of the line. Slaughter-wolf raised his blade to block the strike.

My move was a feint favoured by Trokondas.

I reached out with my right hand, gripped the haft at the butt, and, allowing my left hand to slip down the wood, the blunt end of the head came around like grey lightning.

It was a strike aimed at the joint of the hip, meant to immobilise. Again, the Gautar moved with incredible speed. Somehow he managed to get his sword in the path of my axe, his blade taking the brunt of the force.

I may not have possessed the troll-like power of the champion, but the strike was powerful enough to hurt even a god, and Slaughter-wolf staggered backwards.

"Who are you, Herulian?" Slaughter-wolf growled, no doubt impressed with my skills.

Just then a great cheer went up from the deck of the longships, from the men watching the combat. Atakam's shrill voice cut through the clamour, "Take his head, Son of Attila."

The shaman's words seemed to strike the Gautar like a blow to the chest, and he retreated a step.

"I am Ragnar of the Svear", I growled. "Protector of the Eastern Emperor, vanquisher of the Longobardi and menace to the Goths. And in my veins flows the blood of the great lords of the Sea of Grass."

Slaughter-wolf staggered back another step.

Then he seemed to compose himself, issued a feral roar, and charged.

I felt the burning of the rune of vengeance and my blade came around like lightning. The razor-edge was endowed with the power of the ancients, my strength honed by years of axe-wielding and pulling at the oars. It was a strike that no armour could withstand, powerful enough to sever chain and cleave through flesh and bone.

Slaughter-wolf's speed saved him from being cut in half.

Although my axe shattered his sword, the Gautar was upon me before my blade slammed into his side. His oaken arms closed around my waist and he lifted me off the ground. I slammed my elbow down onto his armoured neck, but it seemed to help naught.

Ten paces farther, Slaughter-wolf tripped and I fell backward, still in the iron embrace of the Gautar. I expected my helmeted head to strike the shingle, but my opponent had carried me into the shallows.

I wished to rise for air but the Gautar was as strong and heavy as three men. He held me fast, pressing my head down onto the slimy bottom. The more I resisted, the stronger his grip became, and I felt myself slipping into the arms of Ran.

But then I felt the burning against my palm and I knew that the old gods were granting me a reprieve. The power of the *Alfars*, the ancient ones, surged through my axe arm. Clutching the head in both hands I struck one last desperate blow.

The stone-honed edge slammed into Slaughter-wolf's helmet and the forged steel split the black plate, stunning the champion. I rose to the surface, gasped for air and saw the lines of Gautar surge forward to assist their unconscious prince.

I had no fight left in me and collapsed, succumbing to the cold embrace of Hella.

Hun shafts slammed into the leading Gautar ringmen. At the same time, I felt powerful hands clasp my shoulders. They dragged me deeper into the ocean, towards the longships.

"At least you've proven that you are no coward", Kursik said as he lifted me up towards the many hands reaching down from the deck.

"No", Abdarakos said as he dragged me onto the timber. "My grandson has proven that he is a fool."

Despite the harsh words, there was no mistaking the pride in the old warrior's voice.

The erilar boomed a command. Oar blades sliced into the black water and the longships shuddered under the power of the rowers.

I raised myself onto unsteady legs and watched the dying pyre recede in the distance.

In a clear challenge, Slaughter-wolf raised his gleaming iron into the sky. "We will meet again, Son of Attila", he roared, and turned away to join his liegemen.

* * *

We rowed through the hours of darkness. Abdarakos offered me a reprieve from pulling at the oars, but I refused and took my turn when it was required.

A few hours later, at the break of day, I sat with Unni, Runa and Atakam while we broke our fast on salted smoked pork, buttermilk and soft cheese.

"Will Slaughter-wolf ever recover from the defeat you have brought upon him?" Unni asked.

Atakam stared at her for a span of heartbeats, then doubled over with laughter.

Unni narrowed her eyes.

Atakam knew better than to rouse the considerable ire of my wife. The old shaman raised an open palm to placate her.

"There will be a verse-maker who travels with Slaughter-wolf", Atakam said. "A poet that takes the coin of the prince. As we speak, the bard will be composing songs and tales to honour his employer's great victory over the marsh-dwelling demons."

"No, child", Atakam said, "the story of Hrothgar and Slaughter-wolf will become legend and his reputation will grow. It is the way of the world."

"What about Ragnar's story and his reputation?" Unni said. "Should we not write down his deeds so that the people will know of his victories?"

Runa then spoke for the first time. "That will not be necessary, child", she croaked, and offered her granddaughter a sweet smile. "The story of Ragnar and your children will live on through the ages, written in the indelible blood of your enemies."

Chapter 13 – Message

An hour before sunset the following day, we pulled our hulls onto the white sand of an isolated beach somewhere in Daneland. It was a pleasant enough evening with almost no wind, so we pitched our tents and sat around roaring driftwood fires.

Most of the warriors who carried no injuries had rowed until the blood from their palms trickled down the shafts of their oars and through the rowlocks. But despite our utter exhaustion, a festive mood was in the air.

I shared a fire with Unni, Kursik, Runa, Beremud and his woman, Maela.

We told tales of the exploits of our friend Boarex, so that the gods would know him when he arrives before the doors of the great hall.

When we had slaked our thirst on the looted ale of Hrothgar, the thick driftwood logs had reduced to glowing embers. My wife unwrapped the last of the fresh meat left over from a wild boar that had fallen to Beremud's spear two days before. I laid the fatty cuts directly onto the glowing coals and soon the air was filled with the aroma of roasting pork.

Later, once we had sated our hunger, I joined the erilar around the cooking fire he shared with Atakam and Sigizan.

"Although we managed to escape the clutches of Hrothgar", Abdarakos said, "we are still in the waters controlled by the Sea Danes. Like wolves, they hunt in packs. Tomorrow I will station two lookouts on the prow of each longship. I will not be caught unawares and fall prey to the Danes again."

"Within four days we will be in the hunting grounds of my brother-in-law, Mourdagos", the erilar added. "Then we no longer have to be on our guard - no Dane will dare enter the waters of the Boat Heruli."

I thought that my grandsire was overly cautious, but kept my counsel.

* * *

Late afternoon, after completing a gruelling shift at the oars, I relaxed for the first time in days, sure that we had managed to evade the local pirates.

"Four *skeids* to the steerboard side!" the lookout boomed, and pointed at the horizon.

Aided by the carved prow beast, I swung up onto the wooden railing to gain a better view. I followed where the sentry pointed and noticed four large longships veer from their course and head straight at us.

On Abdarakos's instruction we donned our armour and strapped on our arms. Then we took the oars from the others to allow them to do the same.

I risked losing the rhythm of the stroke, but stole a glance over my shoulder. The erilar was standing at the prow, his lips pursed and his gaze focused on the approaching ships.

"Archers", he boomed, and the handful of men who followed the way of the bow relinquished their oars to other warriors.

Twenty heartbeats later I stood beside my grandfather. The bow of the khan was in my left fist and three arrows in my draw hand.

"Kill the steersman first", Abdarakos growled, which came as no surprise.

When the approaching ships were two hundred paces away, the erilar nodded to his signifer, who brought a horn to his lips.

Anticipating the command, I drew the sinew string to my ear.

"Stand down", the erilar boomed. The command was so sudden that I nearly released, but somehow I managed to slacken the draw.

Abdarakos slapped me on the back with a giant paw. "Look, Ragnar", he said. "It is Mourdagos."

* * *

Our eight longships were a formidable force. We feared not an attack, and grounded our keels at the nearest suitable beach.

Having set up camp and posted sentries, I went to find the erilar of the Boat Heruli, the grizzled Mourdagos.

The big man lengthened his stride when he noticed my approach, grabbed my head in his hands, and pressed his forehead against mine. "Ragnar, you are welcome at my hearth", he roared in his hearty way, and wrapped an oaken arm around my shoulders. "Come, I have something for you."

I followed him to his cooking fire to find that Abdarakos, Atakam and Sigizan were already there, cross-legged on the furs.

Mourdagos gestured for me to take a seat while a thrall filled our drinking horns with fresh-brewed ale. "Ten days ago, a delegation arrived from the south - Greeks with Ostrogoth guides", he snickered. "Who in their right minds brings Goths into the lands of the Germani?"

The big man took a deep swallow of ale and continued. "Of course, the Goths did not know that the Alemanni and the Franks were at war", he said. "They walked right into the bloody conflict and nearly lost their lives because of it."

"What did they want, Uncle?" I asked, my curiosity roused.

"They were on a mission from the East Roman Empire", Mourdagos said. "And they were looking for you, Ragnar."

I must have frowned.

Mourdagos reached to the side and produced a small walnut chest bound with iron and decorated with silver and gold leaf.

He handed it to me and I nearly dropped it due to the weight.

"Only lead and gold is that heavy", the big man said. "And I would wager that it is not lead."

I unclipped the latch and lifted the lid. Inside, a small velum scroll, adorned with an ornate seal, lay atop gold *solidi* minted in the image of Leo the Thracian.

Greetings, Ragnar of the Heruli

I can only pray to the gods that this letter will reach the far shores of Scandza before it is too late.

On our return to the East, Zeno begged for my forgiveness and embraced Asbadus and me like prodigal sons. But even men with the best of intentions are powerless against the nature of their being.

I need you by my side, Ragnar, as there are few, if any, who can be counted on in the City of Constantine.

I beg you to rush to the Great City and help me thwart the evil that is about to engulf us. Know that time is of the essence - the life of a child is at stake.

Be careful who you trust. The agents of the evildoers are watching for your arrival from the West.

General Flavius Appalius Trokondas

When I was through reading the letter out loud, silence descended upon the gathering.

Everything I was, I owed to the man whose hand had penned the words on the vellum. There was no choice.

"What will you do, Ragnar?" Abdarakos asked, and took a swig from his horn.

"I will stand by my word, Grandfather", I said, "and travel south to the Western Empire. From there I will take ship to the City of Constantine."

Mourdagos shook his head. "The southern lands are in turmoil. The Franks and Alemanni are at each other's throats", he growled, "and besides, by the time that you reach the Middle Sea, it will be late in the season. There will be no captains prepared to take you east."

"I will not be foresworn, Uncle", I said.

The big man reached out and placed a hand on my shoulder, like a father would. "There is a shorter route", he said, but his words were laced with a hesitancy that seemed out of place coming from the lips of the old warhorse.

A frown settled on the brow of Abdarakos. "Do you speak of the route along the *Burichai*, the Deep River?"

Mourdagos issued a grunt of confirmation, and I felt fate tug at my shade.

"I have heard whispers on the Eastwind", Atakam interjected. "The twelve tribes that hold dominion over the lands of *Bazgun* have come west to the banks of the *Burichai*."

"The ancient enemies of Attila", I gasped, having learned about the people who lived north and east of the Dark Sea. "The Saragurs, Barsils and Bulgars are a vicious breed, skilled in the art of war."

"You are silent about the vices of the river, brother", Abdarakos growled, his good eye fixed on Mourdagos.

Mourdagos ignored his brother-in-law and spoke to me instead. "I will accompany you on your journey to the land of the Greeks, Ragnar", he said. "I do not fear the waters of the *Burichai*."

"As will I", Abdarakos growled. "If I am fated to perish, I will meet death with a sword in my hand and a smile on my lips."

"There is no escaping one's fate, Ragnar", Atakam sighed. "I will go as well."

* * *

"I dreamed it", Unni said, when later I told her about the message from Trokondas.

She reached out and pressed her palm against my cheek. "Your journey will be fraught with danger, Ragnar", she added. "Make sure that you return to me before the full moon rises in the fourth month of the new year."

I stared at her like a fool would.

"Why then?" I asked.

Her hand left my cheek to join the other one that was already at a hip.

"It is nine months hence", she said.

"Oh", I replied, and pulled her closer.

Chapter 14 – Burichai (July 474 AD)

Two weeks later.

The Eastern reaches of the Austmarr.

"I hope our women will be safe", Beremud said, his gaze fixed on the eastern horizon far beyond the prow.

"You worry too much", I told my hulking friend, who was no doubt concerned for the welfare of his Frankish wife, Maela. "Sigizan will look after them. He is a warrior of renown."

"What about you, Kauko?" Beremud asked, attempting to find support from the wolfman. "Do you have a woman?"

"Yes", Kauko replied, and carried on sharpening a bone arrowhead.

I observed the exchange with interest, having long before realised that the hunter preferred to communicate with small gestures and only used words as a last resort.

"Do you worry about her safety?" Beremud continued, his way amicable.

"No", Kauko replied without looking up from his toil.

Kursik, who had spent more time in the hunter's presence, came to the rescue. "Long before we were born, all of our fates were carved into the trunk of the world tree", the Hun said, and offered a piece of dried venison to Beremud. "Do you think that you can hide from Hella if she comes for you?"

Beremud accepted the sliver, swallowed it down with a swig of ale, and held out his hand for more. Kursik sliced off a small piece for himself and gave the larger chunk to the Goth.

Beremud tore at the piece with his teeth. "The god-carvings can change fate", he said while chewing, and gestured to Atakam who stood at the prow beside Mourdagos. "The shaman taught you the secrets of the runes, didn't he?"

"There is no need to alter our fates", I said. "Unni and Maela will be safe inside the camp of the Boat Heruli", I added in an attempt to allay my own unspoken fears. "Who will be fool enough to attack a camp full of Mourdagos's warriors?"

Just then Abdarakos hailed me from the steering oar at the stern. As I made my way along the centre aisle, careful to avoid the heaving oars, I stole a glance at the distant shore. It was clear that the erilar had set a course to take us past the tip of a headland jutting out from the south. Our bearing brought us ever closer to the white sandy beach that was backdropped against bright green forests of pine, birch and fir. The coastline was littered with grey-bleached boles of once proud forest giants that had grown too close to the water's edge. I could not help but ponder on what manner of waves had ripped their roots from the earth.

"Do not be fooled, Ragnar", my grandsire said and gestured at the calm sea. "The local tribes believe that when Volos the Deceiver finds the black door unbolted, he crawls up into the world of man. The hairy one soon gets up to his usual mischief and draws the gaze of Perun the Slayer. The god of thunder calls upon the dark clouds in the heavens, that gather upon his command.

Abdarakos pointed at the thick green wall beyond the sandy beach. "Volos is a cunning one and he hides amongst the trees and in the dark water of the fens."

My grandsire gestured with his free hand to accentuate his words. "Then Perun descends from his realm in the sky and commands the wind and water to wake from their slumber. The sea rises up and massive waves pound the treeline to drive Volos from his hiding place. When the battered deceiver emerges into the open, Perun slays the beast with a bolt of lightning and all that he has stolen in the world of man pours down upon the earth as rain."

Before I could reply, Abdarakos gestured with his chin towards the prow.

We rounded the headland and the shore fell away to the south. What little wind there had been suddenly vanished and the surface of the ocean became as smooth as a bronze mirror. It was clear that we had entered the protection of a massive bay.

Due east, I noticed a piece of land rise from the ocean.

"Come, Ragnar, take the oar", Abdarakos said, and I did as I was told.

"Show our steerboard side to the island and ground the hull on one of the beaches to the north", he commanded.

He watched me closely while I manoeuvred the *skeid* according to his words. Every so often he issued a grunt which I believed to be a sign of approval.

Suddenly the erilar stiffened and his hand went to the hilt of his blade. I followed his gaze to where a boat had appeared from behind the island.

"Seal hunters", he said five heartbeats later, breathing a sigh of relief.

I could not help but wonder why the sight of a boat had affected my grandsire so.

Abdarakos was a hard man, not plagued by the weakness of a merciful nature, but he was no fool, and noticed the question in my eyes.

"The mainland over yonder is the domain of the Kurs", he said, and indicated the southern shore, towards the east. "They are a vicious breed, skilled in the art of war and masters of these waters."

Just then the small boat filled with a dozen seal hunters passed fifty paces from our stern. They paid us no heed.

"Do the seal hunters not fear the pirates?" I asked.

"The Kurs endure the seal-hunting peasants because they pose no threat", he said. "When it suits them, the pirates take slaves, skins, or meat as tribute and there is naught the hunters can do."

Abdarakos spat in the water. "The seal hunters are like rats who inhabit the den of a wolf. They feed off the scraps but they are safe from others who would wish to prey upon them."

Suddenly the watchman at the stern shouted a warning, indicating a submerged rock. Without hesitating I pushed the oar to the side to avoid the obstacle. Twenty heartbeats later our keel slid onto the sand and the erilar slapped my shoulder in a sign of approval.

When the warriors had shipped their oars, we jumped off the deck into the waist-deep water and helped to push the longship a few paces onto the beach. There were almost no tides in the Austmarr, so the boat would be safe.

Like the mainland, the island of the seal hunters was overgrown with forests of fir and pine. It was an unknown land, and for that reason we did not venture far from the beach, but made our camp on the sand near the treeline.

By late afternoon we sat beside roaring fires made from the abundance of dry wood.

I stood from the fireside and reached for my bow. "Come, Kursik", I said. "Let us see if there are any boar or deer in these woods."

"Sit, Ragnar", Mourdagos said. "There is no need to go crawling about this foreign island."

"Will we be eating salted fish again?" I asked in return.

Before the big man could offer a reply, I noticed Kauko cock his head and reach for his stone blade.

"Keep a tight leash on the wolf", Mourdagos said, indicating the hunter. "You don't want him to scare away the evening meal."

My uncle had hardly spoken the words when I spied a dozen seal hunters approaching along the sandy beach.

"Peasants cannot resist the allure of gold", Mourdagos sneered. "When the seal hunters saw the glitter of our armour, they knew that we were warriors with bulging purses. Come Ragnar, let us see what the savages wish to exchange for our coin."

Mourdagos, Abdarakos and I met the approaching party fifty paces from our campsite.

An oldster, who appeared to be the leader of the group, stepped forward. The man's skin was brown and wrinkled from a lifetime's exposure to the elements, but his eyes were blue and awake. He was wrapped in seal pelts, and judging by the stench that clung to him, his body had not seen water in many moons.

The peasant regarded us for a handspan of heartbeats while running a calloused hand through his oily, matted black hair. Then he pressed his fist to his chest and thrice repeated an unpronounceable phrase that I took to be his name.

Mourdagos all but ignored the rambling of the seal hunter and produced a coin from his purse.

The oldster's gaze was snared by the coin that Mourdagos turned between his fingers. Then the big man closed his fist around the gold and dropped his arm to his side.

For ten heartbeats the seal hunter seemed to remain under the spell of the gold, unable to tear his eyes away from Mourdagos's hand. Then he snapped out of his reverie as understanding dawned on him. The hunter nodded and issued a broad smile, putting a mouthful of grey-black stumps on full display. He turned to face his men and barked a series of commands.

The old man's underlings presented us with a variety of goods, ranging from vats filled with fresh or pickled seal meat, to soft-worked skins.

My uncle held up two fingers and indicated all the trade goods.

A frown creased the brow of the oldster, who in turn raised a palm and spread out five fingers.

Mourdagos shook his head and countered with an offer of three.

It was clear that they were too far apart. The trade no doubt required a sweetener.

The oldster barked another command and a man appeared from the savages' ranks. He emptied a bag of soft sealskin boots onto the sand. Then he raised four fingers.

Mourdagos clenched the deal with a nod and one by one placed the required coins in the outstretched palm of the seal hunter.

On a signal from the leader, a man with a blonde beard and hair stepped forward from amongst the hunters. The oldster spoke to him for long, gesturing with his hands as was the way of savages.

The blonde man spoke to us in broken Germani. "Lord", he said. "Breidaki wishes to trade again. He wants to know when you will depart."

"We leave the day after tomorrow, one hour after sunrise", Abdarakos replied, making sure to speak slowly so that the man could grasp his words. "We have much gold and wish to purchase more skins."

The blonde man gave the erilar's words to the oldster, who nodded his understanding and indicated for his men to follow him back the way they had come.

Chapter 15 – Kurs

I heaved one of the barrels of seal meat we had bartered for onto a shoulder and stomped back to camp. Burdened by the heavy vessel, my bare feet sank deep into the soft sand. As I strained ahead, I stepped on a concealed rock and a stab of pain shot up my leg. I stumbled, but thankfully managed to keep the contents of the open barrel from spilling.

I bent over at the waist to rub the bridge of my sole and was about to lift the barrel again when I noticed an orange glint. I reached out, pulled the stone from the moist sand, and limped the last few paces back to camp.

"Look", I said, and handed the teardrop-shaped stone to Atakam as I eased myself onto the furs beside the fire.

The old shaman turned the amber in his hand, inspecting it. Then he gestured to the wide waters of the Austmarr. "The local people believe that Perun the Slayer, the mighty god of thunder, built a castle of amber for his comely daughter deep underneath these waves. She displeased her father by falling in love with a mortal man. In a fit of rage, the war god shattered the castle with a bolt of lightning, killing his daughter's lover. Consumed by grief, the goddess vowed to remain amongst the ruins for all eternity. The amber that wash up on these beaches are the remains of the castle", he said, and raised the flawless piece to the light. "But sometimes the tears that the goddess cries are washed ashore. They are precious and priceless."

I nodded and slipped the amber into my purse.

Mourdagos did not listen to the shaman's words – he had other things on his mind.

"Do you think it was wise to share our plans with the savages?" the leader of the Boat Heruli asked his brother-in-law.

My grandsire did not reply immediately, but continued to thread chunks of seal blubber onto a spit iron. Once done, he passed it to Mourdagos, who wound a length of fresh blood pudding around the fat. The big man reached out and carefully rested the iron spit in the forks of branches placed on either side of the fire. Almost immediately the blubber started dripping onto the embers. The fat sizzled and orange flame tongues licked at the grilling sausage, filling the air with an aroma that made my mouth water.

A sly smile appeared on the erilar's lips. "As we speak, the savages are rowing south to inform their masters of our arrival", Abdarakos said. "Now that the seal hunters have profited from barter, they have no further use for us. They will happily trade our lives to the Kurs for a palmful of hacksilver."

The erilar gestured at the bright moon rising in the east. "Tonight, once we have filled our stomachs with seal meat and slaked our thirst with ale, we will strain at the oars and make our way to where the Daugava spills its water into the Austmarr."

Less than two hours later we heaved the longship off the beach. Quietly we slipped our oars through the oarlocks and dipped the wooden blades into the black water. Mourdagos set a relentless pace, intent on reaching the mouth of the river under cover of darkness.

Catching my breath after another gruelling shift at the oars, I stood beside Abdarakos at the stern.

"The Kurs keep a few of their longships at the mouth of the river", my grandfather said. "They allow their allies to row upriver unmolested. From some they extort a heavy tax in gold, amber or furs. Their enemies they put to the blade without question."

"Surely we can use Trokondas's gold to pay the tax", I suggested. "It is the reason why he sent it."

"We are the ones that the Kurs will kill outright", the erilar replied.

I nodded, realising that the Heruli must have had a history with the Kurs.

* * *

An hour before dawn we laid eyes on land. Immediately Abdarakos pulled on the steering oar, and the longship's prow slowly turned to the right, heading south.

When the dark shore fell away, Mourdagos reached down, dipped his hand into the water, and licked a finger. "It is the river", he announced, and in response Abdarakos leaned on the oar and the boat veered to the left, into the mouth of the Daugava.

We hugged the northern bank of the river, and just as the grey, pre-dawn light started to banish the darkness, Abdarakos heaved on the oar and we turned left again, into one of the myriad of side channels. Three hundred paces on, the prow grounded onto a muddy, tree-lined bank.

"Come, Ragnar", Mourdagos said. "Let's see if the seal hunters have betrayed us."

Kauko led Mourdagos, Abdarakos and me across the boggy ground. Eventually, an hour after sunrise, we reached the forested bank of the main channel of the river. On the opposite side of the Daugava, more than three hundred paces distant, seven large longboats were drawn up onto a sandy beach. On the shore beside the ships, trees had been cleared and the roofs of halls were visible above a formidable wooden palisade. The gates of the compound stood wide open, and warriors were moving back and forth between the fort and the longboats.

"They are readying their ships", Mourdagos said.

We did not have to wait long before the longships were pushed into the current. A large *skeid* led the way, heading out into the Austmarr. At the prow, behind a tall, imposing warrior, I noticed the oldster, Breidaki, who we had bartered with. I imagined that I picked up a whiff of his stench on the early-morning breeze.

"The peasant has betrayed us to his masters after all", Mourdagos said, and slapped his brother-in-law's back.

I noticed that his hand came to rest on the hilt of his blade.

"I hope that my path crosses with his again", the big man growled.

"It won't", Abdarakos replied. "When the Kurs find us gone from the island they will open the peasant's stomach and tow him behind the longboat so the creatures of the deep can feast on his innards."

* * *

It was early afternoon by the time we rowed past the camp of the Kurs. Their hatred for the Heruli had caused them to rush away with all their ships. The only thing that the few remaining Kur warriors could do was to shake their fists and shout what we believed to be insults.

"They will be waiting for us on our return", Mourdagos said.

My grandsire shrugged. "Mayhap we are fated to perish in the lands of the East", he said. "Then it matters not."

"The gods favour us", I said. "Because we have managed to evade the Kurs."

The erilar fixed me with a sidelong glance. "If a man manages to sneak past the creatures who guard the gates to the

Underworld, would you consider such a man fortunate?" Abdarakos asked.

"No", I replied.

The erilar issued a grunt then averted his gaze to allow me to come to my own conclusions.

* * *

For many days we struggled upriver, fighting the current of the Daugava through the forested lands of the Semigalliens, Selonians and Latgallians.

Whenever we came across a village, the tribesmen and women were more than happy to trade meat, grain and root vegetables, and receive silver or gold in return.

We continued our journey southeast, the river taking us through sparsely populated lands. Eventually, two weeks after evading the Kurs, the course of the Daugava altered and we found ourselves rowing northeast.

I stood beside Mourdagos at the prow, his eyes scanning the treelined banks.

"We have crossed into the lands of the Sclaveni", Mourdagos said. "They till the soil, but do not be fooled – they are no strangers to war."

Soon the banks of the river abutted green pastures where cattle lazily grazed. The pastures gave way to fields where peasant farmers were toiling to gather the harvest of peas and lentils.

In the distance where the river curved to the north, I noticed a settlement and alerted Mourdagos to the fact.

The big man pursed his lips while running a calloused palm over the weathered oak railing of the longship. "We have taken the *skeid* as far as we can", he said with a hint of sadness in his voice. Then he pointed to the south and east. "The upper reaches of the Deep River, the *Burichai*, lies two days' ride in that direction. We will sell the boat in the town and once we reach the Deep River we will buy another."

The longship was one of the boats we had stolen from Slaughter-wolf. It had been built by the Saxons who were masters at their craft. "Will we be able to buy one of similar quality?" I asked.

Mourdagos issued a snicker of amusement. "With the gold we get for this ship, we will hardly be able to purchase one half its size on the banks of the *Burichai*", he sneered. "The traders always have a reason why it is not a good time to be selling boats. When you wish to buy…, well, then they will find a reason why boats are in short supply."

I have had some experience buying and selling horses and assumed that the same principles applied. Contrary to my assumption, Mourdagos's words would soon be proven wrong.

Chapter 16 – Boat

Not only did we live in troubled times, but the village of the Sclaveni was also on the frontier, bordering the lands of the wild tribes of the north. For that reason, it came as no surprise that the settlement was protected by a fifteen-foot-high wooden palisade.

We rowed towards the bank where a dozen vessels of all shapes and sizes were drawn up onto the sand. Workmen and their slaves scurried about, hammering new planks into place and feverishly caulking seams. The boats that were not under repair were being loaded with supplies. The artisans continued with whatever toil they were engaged in without affording us a second glance.

"It's certainly busier than a few years ago", Mourdagos said with a raised eyebrow.

No sooner had our hull touched the shore when two score of spear-wielding warriors spilled from the crude timber gates and made their way towards us.

Mourdagos jumped down onto the sand and I followed close behind. As the Sclaveni drew near, the big man held his open palms out to the side to show his peaceful intent.

The warriors who approached were tall and muscular. Their loose brown hair hung to their shoulders and thick brown beards covered their faces. All wore knee-length woollen tunics with tight-fitting sleeves. Dark brown baggy breeches protruded from underneath the garments and were tucked into ankle-high brown leather boots. The exposed skin on the back of their hands and forearms were covered with tribal tattoos.

Only their leader wore armour. The nobleman's open face iron helmet was topped with a plume of brown horse hair and sported a sturdy nose guard. Thick chain was riveted onto the rim to protect the back of his neck from a sword strike.

Over his tunic, he wore a short-sleeved leather jerkin that extended to his knees. The entire garment was stitched with small rectangular iron platelets that appeared formidable enough to turn not only a blade but also the tip of an arrow. The iron jerkin was edged with soft leather to ensure that the sharp plates did not eat into his skin.

The nobleman grounded the haft of his iron-tipped spear five paces from us, and I could not help but notice that he was as tall as I was.

"What is your business in the lands of the Sclaveni, Herulian?" the man growled in broken Germani.

"We seek passage to the *Burichai*", Mourdagos replied, his manner curt.

The man regarded us for ten heartbeats and I noticed that he studied my excubitor armour.

"You are on your way to the Empire of the Greeks?" he asked. "I see that your ringman wears the iron of the Romans."

Mourdagos nodded.

"You are welcome in my village, traveller", the Sclaveni said, "but your swords, bows and spears are not."

* * *

Later the same afternoon, I accompanied Mourdagos and Abdarakos into the settlement to seek out a trader who would be willing to pay gold for the longship. Apart from the daggers we had hidden underneath our tunics, we were unarmed.

It did not take long for us to be directed to a longhouse that served as the local drinking establishment. From outside, the roof of the building seemed ridiculously low, but as we entered through the door there were five steps leading downward and I realised that the floor of the house had been sunk into the earth and the walls lined with thick logs.

"It gets cold during winter in these parts", Abdarakos explained when he noticed my surprise.

Inside the spacious longhouse it was remarkably warm thanks to a fire burning brightly in a central hearth and another, supposedly a meal fire, glowing in a far corner. All around, men sat cross-legged on furs beside low tables. Some were laughing and shouting raucously while others conversed in low whispers. Judging by the variety of languages that could be heard, the tavern was no doubt preferred by travellers who made use of the ancient trade route that followed the course of the river.

Abdarakos led us to an empty table near a corner.

Soon a serving girl appeared.

Mourdagos dug into his purse with a thumb and forefinger and placed two silvers in his palm. He mimicked drinking from his empty horn and gestured with cupped fingers into his mouth.

In reply, he received a smile and a nod of understanding.

Sixty heartbeats later, the wench arrived with a large bowl of ale and three joints of smoked boar. Mourdagos passed her another silver which she discreetly secreted into her robe before glancing around to see whether the owner had noticed the windfall.

We filled our horns with golden liquid and settled in for the meal.

While the two older men shared a jest, I took a long draught of ale and reclined with my back against the wall. I could not help but notice that the men at the table next to us spoke Greek. Neither could I prevent their words from reaching my ears.

"There are few ships available, Zachariah", a stocky, black-bearded man said to his companion. "And the ones that are, are not only too small but also trade at three times their value."

The second man reached out and laid a hand on the other's shoulder. "Do not despair, Jacob", he said. "The night is always darkest before the break of day."

"Did I ever tell you what the emperor said when I begged him for justice after our brethren were killed during the riots a few weeks ago, when the synagogue in the copper market was burned to the ground?" the man called Jacob growled. "Do you know that the Greens threw their corpses into the flames?"

Zachariah issued a gasp.

To keep up the ruse that I wasn't listening, I took a swig from my horn and nodded in reply to something Abdarakos said.

"The emperor said that he wished that the Greens had burned the living ones as well", Jacob said, his teeth clenched. "That, to me, was the final straw."

While Zachariah came to terms with the shock caused by Jacob's revelation, I took the opportunity to inform my companions. "Grandfather", I said in the tongue of the Heruli and indicated the two strangers seated at the table close by. "I believe that the gods have sent these two men to us - they are trying to purchase a ship."

Before Abdarakos could reply, Zachariah overcame his shock. "Sometimes I think that it would be better to place ourselves at the mercy of savages like these three", he said to Jacob, and gestured with his chin in our direction. "They are base and boorish but at least they are tolerant of our religion."

"I fear that you are right", Jacob sighed and took a sip of ale.

I turned to face the men and addressed them in the tongue of the Greeks, not using the words of the street vendors and artisans, but that of the upper classes as taught to me by Leodis. "We may be uncouth", I said, "but at least we are gracious enough not to insult strangers – especially men who are easy to anger."

Both Zachariah and Jacob's swarthy complexions turned ashen. For a moment they were too stunned, and I believed, afraid, to reply.

Jews' astuteness at bargaining were well known, and my tactics were deliberate to place them on the back foot. "What would you wish to pay for a good Saxon ship with twenty oars a side?" I asked.

Zachariah swallowed nervously, no doubt worried that we would take whatever they had by force. "Friend", he said, "we have no gold in our purses. Our coin is still with our families who wait with our wagons near the Deep River."

"We wish to sell our ship", I said. "We need the gold to purchase another to journey down the Deep River."

"We can pay no more than two hundred gold coins", Zachariah said, "it is all that we have."

It was clear that their fear of moments earlier had been banished by the smell of possible profit. While I waited for an answer, I allowed my hand to seek the hilt of my dagger and slid it just far enough from the sheath so that they could see the iron of the blade. "You may have gotten away with it once, strangers, but have a care to insult us twice."

Jacob licked his dry lips. "Five hundred is a reasonable price", he said.

"But we wish to inspect your vessel first", Zachariah added.

An hour later we stood on the timber deck of Slaughter-wolf's pride and joy.

Although he tried to suppress it, Jacob found it difficult to hide his pleasure, based on the deal we had concluded.

"I hope that we will be able to afford a boat of similar quality for our passage down the *Burichai*", I said.

Mourdagos waved away my concerns. "You have done better than we believed possible, Ragnar", he said, patting my shoulder. "And if they have cheated us, well… then we open their throats, don't we?" he grinned, putting his filed teeth on full display.

I nodded and translated the big man's words for the benefit of our guests.

Chapter 17 – Thirteenth tribe

The following morning, Jacob and Zachariah arrived early, in the company of a Sclaveni guide.

The erilar agreed that five of his warriors would remain on board to guard our ship while the rest of us travelled seventy miles overland to the banks of the *Burichai*.

Although the Sclaveni were not people of the horse, we managed to lay our hands on twenty mounts and a dozen pack animals. It meant that some of us were forced to go on foot, but at least the purchase of the mules ensured that no one carried any baggage.

Abdarakos showed his cunning by coercing Jacob and Zachariah to open their purses when the horse trader demanded payment. The Jews would require the use of the animals on their return journey in order to transport their families to our ship moored in the Daugava. They both agreed, on condition that they would be afforded the use of two horses.

"Where will you go?" I asked Jacob, who rode abreast of me.

"Our religion requires every man to study our holy book", he said.

I nodded, as I had heard about the people who pray to only one God.

"That means that all Jewish men, even the boys, are literate", Jacob said. "Have you ever heard of a people where all the men are able to read, write and work numbers?"

"No", I replied earnestly.

"My people will go and live with the, er…, barbarians", he said with half a smile. "Our artisans will apply their skills, while others will help the barbarian lords keep records of their trade and their coin."

"Which tribe?" I asked.

"Anyone who will take us in", he replied. "We will help them to bring order to their domain, and in turn, I hope, they will respect and appreciate us. Not like the Romans who take us for granted and accuse us of whispering blasphemies every time we honour our God."

* * *

The area through which we journeyed was under the firm control of the Sclaveni. Of the usual brigands who preyed on travelling traders there were no sign, as few robbers in their right mind would attack a band of Heruli warriors. Or so I believed.

On the fourth day of slogging along the muddy track, there was a disturbance up ahead.

Kursik, Beremud and I, who were riding in the vanguard of our column, went to investigate.

We found two of Abdarakos's oathsworn at the side of the path. Their horses had been taken, and one of our scouts nursed a wound to his leg where a spear had pierced the flesh. Nearby lay the corpses of three brigands who wore the garb favoured by the Sclaveni.

It was evident that the scouts had been ambushed so there was no need for lengthy explanations.

"How many and which way did they go?" I asked while we strung our bows and loosened our blades in our scabbards.

"Ten remain, lord. Few wear armour", the wounded man replied and pointed at a spot where the undergrowth had been trampled.

We spurred our horses into the greenwood.

I have heard men say that amongst trees and through undergrowth, a mounted man cannot move as fast as a warrior on foot. Such men are fools for they have never seen a Hun and his mount weave through the forest.

In less than a quarter part of an hour, I noticed Kursik drop his reins and draw the bowstring to his ear. His release was followed by a scream.

If the brigands had the clarity of mind to flee in different directions, at least half of them would have survived. Believing that there is some kind of strength in numbers, they remained together as a band. When they eventually made a stand, our arrows had whittled them down to five.

We thundered down on the robbers. Kursik's battle-axe whirred through the air and embedded in the unarmoured torso of a man who stepped forward to slash at him with a rusty blade. I took a spear strike on my armour and smashed the blunt end of my axe into the skull of a brigand as I passed.

Beremud was right behind me. As I turned to attack again, I saw his horse slam into the last three remaining men. One was killed instantly, I believe, while the others staggered backwards. Before they could recover, the big Goth's heavy axe flashed twice.

While Beremud took their heads, I walked over to the broken body of the man who had been struck by the horse. To my surprise he was still breathing. I noticed that although his armour and clothes had seen better days, it was of good quality. There was no doubt in my mind that he had long before been a lord of men.

He turned his head so he could look me in the eye. "My neck is broken", he stammered in passable Greek. "I beg you to put my sword in my fist and send me on my way."

Three paces from us, a well-forged weapon lay amongst the underbrush. I took his lame hand in mine, lifted it so that he could see, and closed his fist around the jewel-encrusted pommel.

I drew my dagger.

"I was not always a man who preys on travellers, stranger", he said, and issued a wry smile. "My people lived far to the south, on the eastern bank of the *Burichai* bordering the domain of the clans of the land of *Bazgun*."

He broke into a coughing fit and I noticed specks of frothy blood in his beard.

"I know of the twelve tribes", I said. "Did the Saragurs drive you from your lands?"

The most his crushed spine allowed was an almost imperceptible shake of the head, and I am certain that he regarded me with pity in his eyes. "Beware the thirteenth tribe", he croaked, and a shudder racked his broken body.

"Send me to my forefathers, warrior", he whispered, and closed his eyes. "I can see them, they are waiting for me on the other side."

I nodded, and did what needed to be done.

* * *

"He mentioned another tribe – a thirteenth", I said, and used the tip of my dagger to spear a chunk of grilled boar from the coals.

"Did the brigand speak their name?" Atakam asked.

"No", I replied.

"Many times I have heard travelling merchants mention warlike races that live beyond the Belt of Stone", the shaman said and gestured to the east. "Sometimes great battles or terrible droughts drive them west, through the treacherous passes."

"The troubles of the Sclaveni do not concern us", Mourdagos said. "We will beach our hulls on the western bank of the *Burichai* to avoid contact with the tribes."

Having addressed my concerns, the big man struck up a conversation with Abdarakos and Atakam who sat beside him, and paid me no further heed.

"Did you travel north along the Deep River?" I asked our two guests, using the Greek tongue.

"We have been on the road for many months", Zachariah replied. "We commissioned a boat in the City of Constantine and sailed north along the western bank of the Dark Sea to the mouth of the Deep River. There, we purchased ox wagons and trundled north along the western bank of the river."

"Why did you not sail up the Deep River by boat?" I asked.

Jacob regarded me like one would the village idiot. "We asked around", he said. "And all we spoke to cautioned against using the river."

I raised an eyebrow. "Why?" I asked.

Zachariah first made sure that none were listening. Then he leaned in closer and lowered his voice, "All said that only madmen and fools are stupid enough to travel by boat along the Deep River."

Chapter 18 – Smola

"How far to the Deep River?" I asked Mourdagos.

He gestured to a grey smog that slowly drifted along the ravine at the bottom of the nearby hill, obscuring the thick boles of age-old pines bordering the track. "The town on the banks of the *Burichai* is called Smola", he said. "We are almost there."

He had hardly uttered the words when we descended into the smoky mist. Immediately my nose and throat were assaulted by the overwhelming stench of pine tar.

"See", he said, and indicated something at the side of the road.

I squinted into the fog and noticed bands of peasants toiling around what could only be tar pits.

"Smola is the Sclaveni word for pitch", the big man explained. "These men make a good living off pine tar. It is in demand."

"Why would one need to make such preparations for gliding along a river?" I asked.

A frown creased Mourdagos's brow and for a span of less than a heartbeat I thought I noticed a glimpse of trepidation in the big man's eyes. But then it was gone, and I dismissed it because I knew that my uncle feared naught.

"You will see", he said, and nudged his horse to a canter.

* * *

"My father named me Ratislav, he did, lord", the oldster said, closed one of his nostrils with a thumb, and blew a blob of snot into the shallow water around his feet before wiping off the remains with a food-stained sleeve. "But I've never wielded iron, lord, so here, up and down the Deep River, they call me Bogdan, they do." He paused again to snort mucus back up his nose. "You see, lord", he continued, "the men who pay me gold all say that that I am a gift from the gods."

The guide issued a smile to emphasize the fact that the gods favoured him, and I was surprised to see that his teeth were in good condition. Almost immediately he went into a coughing fit, cleared a piece of troublesome phlegm from his throat, and spat it out.

He was clever enough to realise that no lord would wish to share a deck with a man afflicted with some coughing sickness or other. "It's the pine tar and the smoke that affects my chest, lord", he said by way of explanation. "The ailment goes away as soon as Smola disappears around the first bend in the river, it does."

Abdarakos eyed the man critically. "How many times have you been down the river?" the erilar asked.

"I do three trips every season before the *Burichai* freezes over, I do, lord", he said. "I've been doing it since I was twelve years old, lord. I've seen more than fifty summers, I have."

He refrained from providing the requested number, and stared at us with a blank expression. I was convinced that he was unable to work the sums in his mind.

"More than a hundred times", I told my grandsire.

"We will take you", Abdarakos said to Bogdan. "But if you have deceived us and your cough remains, I will open your throat with my own blade."

The old river guide nodded his thanks. "Four gold coins to get you safely to the Dark Sea", he said. "But I need two in advance, I do", he said. "So that my woman can feed herself while I'm away, lord."

"Six", Abdarakos growled and Bogdan's eyes grew wide with greed. "But only when we reach the shores of the sea. Your woman is no concern of mine."

"Thank you, lord, I will sort out the old hag, I will, lord", the guide croaked, and again succumbed to a coughing fit.

Having arranged the services of a guide, my grandsire and I strolled further along the bank to where Mourdagos and Atakam were speaking with someone. The man, no doubt a boatbuilder, held a small adze in his hand, which he used to gesture at the half dozen river boats on the shore behind him – all in varying stages of completion.

When we joined them, they were making their way towards a twenty-pace-long ship. Close by, thralls were adding what appeared to be tree roots to a large copper cauldron filled with boiling pine tar. Other workmen, possibly apprentices, were tying the overlapping planks together with cooled-off lengths of root that had been braided into rope.

"I use only alder roots to bind the planks", the shipwright said with pride, and ran his hand along the curve of the prow. "All my prows and sterns are made from a single piece of spruce", he added and indicated with his adze. "See, this part is from the root and this is the lower trunk."

Then he leaned in as if imparting a secret. "I have dealt with travellers who are willing to settle for a prow that is made of pine or joined timber", he whispered. "Sometimes their bones wash up on the banks when the snow melts."

"We will take this one", Mourdagos said.

"Five hundred gold coins", the shipwright replied and folded his heavily muscled arms across his chest.

It was Mourdagos's turn to lower his voice. "We have been told of the troubles downriver, boatbuilder", he said. "And we know that the tribes are restless. How many boats have you sold this season?"

"Four hundred and fifty", the man countered. "It is the best I can do."

"Four hundred", Mourdagos said, and showed the shipwright the glitter of his coin.

* * *

Come evening, we all congregated around a fire. Earlier in the day, Jacob and Zachariah had been reunited with their families and we had said our goodbyes.

I was surprised when Jacob arrived at the fireside.

"I have a boon to ask, lord", he said to Mourdagos, who, with an open palm, indicated that he should join us around the fire.

"The boat we have purchased from you is not large enough to take both my and Zachariah's extended family", he said.

My uncle acknowledged his words with a nod, while taking a swig from his horn.

"Zachariah and I have decided that he will take his family north to see whether he can find a place where we can settle", Jacob said. "My family will remain in Smola for the time being, until Zachariah calls for us."

"If the Fates do not smile on Zachariah, at least you and your family will survive", Abdarakos growled. "It is a sensible plan, but what has it got to do with us?"

Jacob inclined his head, acknowledging that the erilar's question was to be expected. "Tar is a valuable commodity in the City of Constantine", he said. "There it sells for many times the value that one pays in this settlement. Some of my kinsmen have chosen to remain in the Great City and I wish to take a few barrels of this pine tar south to see whether the shipwrights will be willing to purchase it."

"You may join us", Mourdagos said.

A frown settled on Jacob's brow. "How much will you charge me?" he asked.

The big man issued a grunt of amusement. "Nothing, of course", he replied. "The Heruli do not extort gold from men to whom we have extended hospitality."

* * *

For days we rowed downriver through hill country. The banks of the Deep River were heavily forested for the most part, except for the occasional swamp, or where Sclaveni farmers were scratching out a living from small cleared fields.

Whenever I looked, I noticed Bogdan reclining against his furs. I watched him while I pulled on the oar - most of the time he seemed to be sleeping while on other occasions he studied the far bank through slitted eyes. I could not help but to be irritated by the oldster who, I was convinced, was an expense without any benefit. At least, I thought, he had not lied about his ailment, because he had not so much as coughed once after we left Smola.

"We are wasting our gold on the guide", I dared to say one evening around the fire.

Mourdagos met my gaze. "The river is not what it seems, Ragnar", he said. "Wait until we reach the Dark Sea before you place a value on the old man."

The big man's words filled me with a sense of foreboding, but it soon proved that the river would not be our only source of concern.

Chapter 19 – Kyiv

Mid-afternoon on the tenth day on the river, Bogdan seemed to suddenly wake up from his interminable slumber. The guide slowly gained his feet, then made his way to the stern where Abdarakos was teaching me the finer points of being a helmsman.

"Lord", the oldster said, and pointed at the eastern bank. "Before the sun sets tonight the river will leave the hills and trees behind. Soon we will emerge onto the plains – the Wild Fields of the nomads. It will be better if you stay closer to the western bank once we leave the hill country."

My grandsire gestured towards a small sandy area visible on the eastern bank, a few hundred paces downstream. "Take us there, Ragnar", he said. "Let us hunt for the pot while we still can."

There was a reason for him choosing the eastern bank. We had long before realised that game animals like boar and deer were more plentiful across the river, probably because there were fewer men who hunted on the far shore.

Abdarakos turned to the guide. "Do not fear", he said. "Tonight we will make our camp on the western bank."

The erilar's words seemed to placate the guide, who returned to the spot where his furs were stacked against the board.

As soon as our keel slid onto the sand, Kursik, Beremud, Kauko and I ventured into the greenwood in an attempt to bolster our supplies. By then we had learned to allow my wild friend to lead the way. Less than a mile into the hinterland, Kauko, who was twenty paces ahead of us, raised an open palm and went down into a crouch. We remained where we were, allowing him to reconnoitre the area up ahead.

Two hundred heartbeats later, Kauko emerged behind us, nearly causing me to issue a yelp. The wild man bared his teeth, which I had learned was his attempt at a grin, and held up both hands, the fingers spread. "So many horses. All blue", he whispered. "One warrior."

Kauko's words caught me off guard. I had not expected to encounter horsemen in the forest.

I was about to lead the way to question the man who was watching over the horses when an old memory surfaced. "The *Kügel*", I mouthed.

My words were not lost on Kursik, a snarl appearing on the Hun's scarred face. "Riders of the blue roans", he sneered.

Years before, on the night of my birth, the horde of the Saragurs had overran the camp of the Huns. Atakam told me that he and Sigizan had returned to the place of destruction, only to find that the savage horsemen had left not a single living thing alive. Women, oldsters and children were all put to the blade. Even the horses, goats and chickens had been slaughtered. Near the place he had found the body of my mother, where her bodyguards had made their last stand, the ground was littered with the carcasses of blue roan horses – the mounts favoured by the clan of the *Kügel*.

Kauko's eyes remained on me, like a tame wolf waiting for his master's orders. The presence of my mother's murderers caused a rage to rise like bile. I met the wild man's gaze and drew a finger across my throat.

I had long ago realised that Kauko had no qualms about taking a life. He issued an offhanded nod, as if I had asked him to pass the wine, and melted into the undergrowth.

We followed twenty heartbeats later, only to find our wild friend rummaging through the saddlebags of the now unguarded mounts. To one side, the feet of a corpse poked from the shrubbery. I noticed the wild man discard a jewelled armband, rather opting to pocket a round of hard cheese, again confirming that his kind placed no value on coin and trinkets.

Kursik and I strung our bows and Beremud hefted his heavy axe.

"Find them", I said to Kauko, who nodded in acknowledgement, and led us deeper into the greenwood. Less than a mile farther he halted, his gaze focused on something up ahead. Crouching, we made our way to his side.

Twenty paces in front of us, in a small clearing, nine *Kügel*s surrounded three Sclaveni boys and one young woman. All of them had been tied to saplings - their hands bound behind their backs, while broad leather straps tightly secured their necks to the trunks.

A *Kügel* warrior unsheathed his dagger, took a step closer to one of the boys, and drew the blade along the side of the captive's face. The boy issued a whimper and the savages erupted in raucous taunting and laughter.

The woman issued a curse of anger and defiance, causing the knife-bearing savage to turn on her.

In that moment I felt as if the gods had taken me back twenty years, and it was as if I was witnessing the horrors that had played out in the camp of the Huns when the Saragur horde had attacked.

Before I could stop myself, my bearded axe was in my fist and I was sprinting towards the savages, whose backs were turned to me. It is not my way to kill a man from behind, but the *daemon* of vengeance had taken hold of me and I struck down the knife-wielding *Kügel* with a vicious blow, the blade of my axe biting deep into the vulnerable place where the base of the neck meets the shoulder.

The tempered edge was keen as a razor, and cut clean through flesh and bone. The man beside the knife-wielder turned to face the threat, his sword halfway out of the scabbard. He got no further before the flat of my axe head struck the side of his helmet, shattering his skull with a sickening crunch, and sending the corpse careening into the underwood.

The third warrior managed to bring his blade to bear, but it helped him naught. I parried his slash, winded him with a strike from the butt, and took his arm off at the elbow with a cut that would have made Trokondas proud.

By then, the other six warriors had regained their wits.

Two warriors rushed me.

I chose the one nearest. He tried to parry my swing with his curved sword, but I was strong as an ox from pulling a heavy oar for weeks on end. The blade of my axe cut through the warrior's leather armour and the iron bit deep into his chest. I swung around to face the other, but one of Kursik's three-bladed arrows slammed into the *Kügel's* neck.

And then Beremud was at my side.

Although the Saragurs were formidable horse warriors, on foot they were no match for three men who had served in the ranks of the excubitors. Two more fell to our blades before the last two remaining *Kügels* dashed into the undergrowth in an attempt to escape certain death.

Kauko slipped his stone blade from its sheath and trotted after them.

The four Sclaveni stared at us, no doubt uncertain whether the Fates were smiling or frowning on them.

I pulled my dagger and cut their bonds.

Judging by their clothes and bearing, they were nobles. For that reason I addressed them in the tongue of the Greeks. "I am Ragnar of the Svear", I said. "Why are you pursued by the *Kügel*?"

It was the woman who answered. "We come from a village four days' ride to the south", she said. "My father's warband was defeated by the warriors of the Clan of the Blue Roan", she sneered. "The villagers who were not taken as slaves had their throats opened. My grandfather and mother gave their lives so my brothers and I could ride away and escape the savages."

Before I could reply, Kauko arrived, dragging a Saragur corpse by the leg. He dumped the dead body unceremoniously. "Other one got away", he said. "He had a horse."

"The *Kügel* scum has stolen one of our horses", a boy, no older than sixteen, spat. "The filth who has escaped will bring his kin and hunt us down."

"Not if you go to the other side of the Deep River", I said. "I believe there is no place for a horseman to cross for at least a hundred miles."

"I will not run from the ones who have slaughtered my people", he growled. "I will make a stand and die a warrior's death."

"There is a fine line between bravery and stupidity", I said. "Make a home for you and your brothers and your sisters. Gather warriors under your banner, and when you are strong, fall upon your enemy when they least expect it."

"You are not alone, young warrior", I growled. "My mother died by a *Kügel* blade."

"How long did you wait?" the boy sneered.

I used by reddened axe to point at the Saragur corpses. "More than twenty years", I replied.

My answer seemed to mollify the young man. His sister walked over to him, put her arm around his shoulders, and whispered into his ear, drawing a nod from the boy.

"I will give heed to your words, warrior", the boy replied. "But to the gods I swear – I will have my revenge."

* * *

An hour later we waved goodbye to Kie and his three siblings.

They stood on the high western bank above the blue water of the Deep River, backdropped against the lush green forest that covered the hills behind them.

"I wonder whether they will have peace or war?" I mused.

"That, Ragnar, is for the gods to decide", Atakam replied and turned his gaze to the south.

Chapter 20 – Do not sleep

We followed Bogdan's advice and set a course that hugged the western bank.

Despite our guide's concerns, we sighted no hostile riders, but our good fortune came to an abrupt end early afternoon on the fourth day after the run-in with the *Kügel*.

Just after vacating my seat at the end of my rowing shift, Kauko came to stand beside me at the ale vat. "Do not look", he said. "Riders watch from amongst the trees."

I dunked my horn into the ale and chugged the contents. Although I scanned the eastern bank from the corner of my eyes, I faked staring at the prow. It turned out to be a fruitless exercise because I spied no movement.

Kauko noticed that I failed to spot the riders and issued a snort of derision. "Twice a double handful. Hidden in the beech thicket."

Trying not to be obvious, I did as I was told, this time noticing the faint shapes of horsemen.

"How long have they been trailing us?" I asked.

"Since sunrise", he said. "Then there were five."

Before I could mention it to my grandfather or Mourdagos, I felt the ship swerve sharply, moving even closer to the western bank. Abdarakos was at the steering oar. Beside him stood our guide who appeared to be more alert than I had ever seen him before.

So focused was I on the horsemen that, at first, I failed to pick up on the faint roar coming from up ahead. As we drifted downstream, the roar became louder and I noticed that the entire width of the river was blocked by sharp rocks that protruded from the surface like incisors from the jaw of a monstrous creature. Around the teeth of stone, the water foamed white, reminding me of the maw of a rabid beast.

I felt my stomach constrict with fear.

The old guide noticed my trepidation. "They call it *Do not Sleep*", he cackled, and pointed at the grey stones on the riverbank that marked the graves of many interred victims. "There lie the ones who slept."

The erilar guided the ship closer to the shore. When we felt the keel touch the sandy bottom, he ordered all of us to disembark.

Bogdan retrieved a canvas bag from amongst his possessions and shook ten lengths of rope onto the timber deck. With great care he tied the ropes to the railing and lowered the loose ends through the oarlocks, five on each side.

Then, without a moment's hesitation, the old guide called out ten names, the largest and strongest of the warriors. As I waded into the water to take up a rope, I realised that I had underestimated the guide. He had not been asleep after all.

Abdarakos took the steering oar while Mourdagos stood at the prow.

Twenty paces ahead, Bogdan waded through the waist-high water, guiding us through a maze of submerged rocks that were ragged enough to rip open the planking of even the stoutest boat.

On the guide's signal we pulled on the ropes, and the ship slowly started to move forward. As we drew closer to the foaming maw of the beast, the water jerked violently at the hull. It required all of our collective strength to keep the ship on the path set by Bogdan.

At one point he indicated for us to stop, and we strained against the current to halt the heavy boat. Judging by the expression on our guide's face, I knew that the danger was at its greatest. He allowed us to catch up with him, and placed a hand on the thick alder beam at the prow, guiding us this way and that as we battled with the unwieldy ship. The rushing river made it difficult to see, but there were times when the water cleared for only a heartbeat. Then I spied the hidden teeth of the beast that were waiting patiently, ready to devour the boat and the shades of men who erred.

When we emerged safely on the other side of the rapids, we let go of our ropes and issued cheers of victory.

Bogdan turned around, a frown furrowing his brow. "Do not celebrate too soon, lord", he said. "Six still remain."

We negotiated the second and third set of obstacles in much the same way.

It was when we emerged onto the calm waters at the far side of the third that I noticed not a roar, but rather a sound akin to thunder.

"We will soon come to the place where the river giant grinds the stones together, lord", Bogdan said, and pointed at the fog rising in the distance. "The insatiable one makes the sky thunder, and shakes the banks of the Deep River."

"He has always been there, lord", he said. "And it doesn't matter how many shades he claims, he is never content."

Bogdan turned to face Abdarakos at the oar. "We cannot pull the boat through the Grandfather Rapids, lord", he said. "We will have to cut logs and move the boat across the land."

"How far?" the erilar asked.

"Five miles, lord", the guide said. "It will take six days. The path is difficult."

My grandsire thought on the guide's words for a span of heartbeats.

"Can we negotiate the rapids with the ship?" he asked. "I have heard men say that it can be done."

For twenty heartbeats Bogdan failed to reply, as if he wished not to utter the answer that followed. "It can be done, lord", he said reluctantly. "My father showed me the path, lord, but…", for a few moments he struggled to find the words, "… but the river giant is fickle, lord."

"How long to cross by boat?" Mourdagos asked.

"Two hundred heartbeats, lord", the guide replied. "But I must take the oar, lord."

* * *

While half of the crew, along with most of our baggage, circumvented the rapids on foot, we rowed downstream. Apart from the thundering roar, there was little evidence of the white waters that we knew lay ahead.

"The water is calmer than I thought it would be", Beremud said from across the aisle while pulling on his oar.

He had hardly uttered the words when the hull shuddered. Moments later the ship gained speed, as if a god had picked up an invisible rope and hauled us towards the white water up ahead.

Bogdan leaned on the steering oar and my grandsire helped him to fight the powerful water. The ship headed for the middle of the river, and for a heartbeat I thought that the old man was intentionally guiding us to our doom. But the current took us and propelled the ship through a channel so narrow that I heard the rocks shave at the planking of the hull.

We had hardly passed the obstacle when he pulled on the oar, taking us closer to the western bank. The ship bucked like a wild horse, but we managed to clear yet another set of rocks.

Again, he leaned on the oar and shouted to Abdarakos, to be heard above the thunder of the water. "Help me take her across the river, lord", he said. "We have to pass through the Gates of Hell near the far bank."

Even with my grandsire's great strength added to that of the guide's, I could see that they struggled to overcome the brutal power of the current pulling us towards the jaws of the beast.

We strained against the oars to level the ship, fighting the roaring river that threatened to rip the hafts from our fists.

"Nearly there, lord", Bogdan shouted, half a smile visible on his weathered face.

And then our doom unfolded in full view.

I was grinning back at the smiling guide when an arrow slammed into his temple, passed through his skull, and exited above the ear on the other side of his head. The corpse slumped forward, ripping the steering oar from my grandsire's grasp. But Abdarakos lunged at the haft and managed to get a hand on the wood before the power of the river tore it free of its leather bindings that affixed it to the timber. With godlike strength, the erilar strained at the oar. He battled the raging water and managed to steady the boat.

As one, a sigh of relief escaped the lips of the men at the oars. Then I noticed Abdarakos's eyes grow wide with fear.

Before I could turn my head to glance over my shoulder, the ship slipped over the edge of a roaring abyss. For a span of time that felt like three heartbeats, I found myself staring up at the dark grey clouds. The impact that followed was akin to falling from the saddle under full gallop and striking the stones of a Roman road. The oar was torn from my fist and I tumbled backwards along the deck - my ears filled by the screams of the men and the sound of shattering timber.

The river sucked me down, and although I swallowed water, I managed to draw air into my chest. Something hit me against the side of the head, but I kept my wits about me. The next moment there was solid ground beneath my feet, and with the last power in my legs I propelled myself up towards the light. I broke the surface of the raging river and thanked the gods for affording me another breath.

A moment later the river calmed and I spied Kursik floating facedown in the grey water close by. I reached him in two strokes, turned his body over, and noticed that he wasn't drawing breath. In desperation I took him in an embrace so that his head rested on my shoulder, then struck three enormously powerful blows to his back with the flat of my hand.

Kursik's shade regained his body. I felt warmth on my back as his lungs expelled the water from his chest. Again, I heard the roar of the river beast up ahead and struggled against the renewed tug of the current. I turned my friend onto his back, and, keeping hold of him with one hand, used my legs and free arm in a desperate effort to gain the eastern bank.

No matter how hard I kicked and pedalled, the god of the river was just too powerful. I was but ten paces from the bank when I felt the last of my strength fade away. I clenched my teeth and went beyond the threshold of pain and exhaustion, but it helped me naught. For the second time that day I felt Hella pull me down into her cold realm. I kept an arm clenched around Kursik's neck and clawed at the disappearing surface with the other. Then my fist closed around something solid and I realised that it was a rope of sorts. Slowly we were dragged to the safety of the bank, the identity of our saviour obscured by the mogshade.

As soon as I felt solid ground underneath my feet I stumbled onto the bank, my back facing the trees, dragging the Hun behind me. But I was wearier than I had ever been. I slipped in the mud and fell down heavily with a half-conscious Kursik landing on top of me.

Keeping my eyes closed, I mouthed a prayer to Ulgin for delivering us from certain death.

Then I heard voices mutter in the tongue of the Sea of Grass. Dazed, my eyes followed the rope that was still clenched in my fist and I noticed that the other end was tied to a rider's saddle.

And then a blue roan emerged into the daylight.

Chapter 21 – Coward

I threw the braided rope from my fist, but another lasso snaked out from the shadows of the greenwood and a noose tightened around my neck. Violently, I was plucked to my feet and I would have been strangled there and then if I had failed to get both hands on the leather.

With the cruel laughter of *Kügel* warriors resonating in my ears, I was half-dragged along for fifty paces and left sprawling in a clearing.

Slowly I regained my senses.

"If we are fortunate, they will sell us as slaves", someone croaked, and I barely recognised the voice as belonging to Beremud. "But I think these ones just want us for sport."

"It would have been better had the river taken us", Kursik growled softly from my other side.

For a moment I felt guilty for saving his life.

"A mongrel dog that still breathes is better than a dead lion", Jacob admonished the Hun in his broken version of our tongue.

"When the *Kügel* have taken your skin, eyes and tongue and begin to work on you with fire, you will speak differently",

Kursik sneered in reply, but the Hun was silenced by a strike from a spear haft.

While they trussed us up, I took time to study our captors. The Saragur warriors' hair, like their beards, were ruddy brown and tied back in single, long braids. Their armour was forged from iron and favoured scales for turning arrows, although I noticed the odd piece of plate and chain. Their riveted helmets were open-faced, of the conical type, and sported plumes of horse hair. Their braccae were loose-fitting, tucked into soft undyed leather boots made for men who spend their days in the saddle.

Once the *Kügel* were ready, they tied us to the harnesses of their packhorses, like one would do with goods. While his men secured me to the back of a gelding, one of the riders, who was no doubt their leader, turned to face me.

"Our Khan, Kubrat, sent his only son to track down the spawn of the Sclaveni chieftain who fled after we defeated them in battle", he said. "But Kubrat's boy was killed by someone who keeps the company of Huns", he added and turned to face another rider.

"Is the one who murdered chief Kubrat's boy one of them?" he sneered.

Without hesitation the warrior pointed at me. "It was that one, Lord Kul", he replied, his tone flat.

The man seemed familiar. I recognised him as the warrior who had fled into the forest days before when we stumbled upon the *Kügel* warband.

The leader's lips split into a blood-curdling sneer. "Make sure no harm comes to this one", he said, and stroked my hair like one would a favourite hound. "Kubrat will pay us well for the chance to get him under the blade."

* * *

For close on two days the Saragur warband travelled east, into the lands of *Bazgun*. We were treated as loot, as valuable baggage, and apart from an occasional strike from a tamarisk shaft meant to silence us, we remained unharmed.

Until the second evening on the road, that is.

The *Kügel* set up their camp at the bottom of a shallow ravine, under the cover provided by a birch thicket. Beremud, Kursik, Jacob and I were firmly secured – each to a trunk. We were fed and allowed to relieve ourselves under the watchful eyes of our captors, their spearpoints trained on us.

The leader of the warband, Kul, was a careful, meticulous man. Throughout the night a guard was stationed close by to ensure that we did not get up to mischief. Although the Saragurs draped furs around our shoulders, the night was hellishly cold and I struggled to sleep, preferring to waste my time straining against the bonds until the rope ate into my flesh and I felt the hot blood run into my clenched fists.

Eventually I succumbed to exhaustion.

I woke when I heard an intake of breath, followed by a soft gurgle – the sound made when frothing blood escapes an opened throat.

Three paces away, I noticed a dark shape lower the body of the dead guard onto the carpet of leaves.

The man moved into the faint light cast by the last of the glowing embers, black liquid dripping from the blade in his fist. "You have killed my lord", he growled.

"You ran like a coward", I replied. "Do you really believe that you will regain your honour if you kill me?"

The warrior's lips curled back in a sneer. "No", he said. "But my khan will never know that I ran away and left his son to his fate if there is no one to relate the tale."

He had a point.

To my surprise he bent down, and using the corpse's robe, wiped the blood from the dagger. He picked up the warrior's spear, which he used to indicate the prone body. "You killed him", he said. "And when I arrived to take over the watch, I caught you in the act."

Beremud must have woken up while the warrior spoke.

"Then you will have to kill us all", my friend growled.

The white of the *Kügel's* teeth visible in the slivers of moonlight betrayed his smile of affirmation.

He hefted the spear.

From the darkness beyond, a battle-axe whirred and slammed into the skull of the helmetless warrior. His eyes rolled back in their sockets and the corpse slumped forward, coming to a rest across my half-frozen legs.

The leader of the warband stepped into the small circle of light and spat on the corpse. "Coward", he sneered. "I wondered why he lived while all the others died by your blades."

Then he picked up his fallen comrade and left the body of the coward where it lay.

Another guard made his appearance and I drifted off to sleep, the last warmth seeping from the fur-clad corpse providing some measure of respite from the terrible cold.

* * *

Come morning, the leader woke us and heaved the stiff corpse from my aching legs with a booted foot.

Kursik and Jacob, who had slept through the whole affair, stared at the dead man with eerily similar frowns furrowing their brows.

"It's a long story", Beremud said, and received a spear haft to the back as a reward.

We were valuable to the warriors as they would trade us for gold. Each of us were given a cup of heavily salted, heated mare's milk before being loaded onto the packhorses.

Mid-morning we were moving across rolling hills when an outrider returned. He reined in close to the leader of the band, his horse frothing at the mouth. "Lord Kul", he said, his eyes wide with fear. "An Avar raiding party is riding this way."

I exchanged glances with Kursik as I was unfamiliar with the tribe, and received a shrug in reply.

It took less than a heartbeat for Kul to mirror the expression of the scout. "Did they see you?" he asked, his eyes already scanning the surrounding hills.

"No, lord" the scout replied.

Kul breathed a sigh of relief and twisted in the saddle to issue instructions to his men.

Behind him, to the left, I noticed a glint as the sun reflected off burnished metal. Moments later, a lone horseman appeared on the far horizon. By the time Kul turned around, he was gone.

For a span of heartbeats, I toyed with the thought of warning our captors. But then I thought of the words that Leodis, my Greek mentor, used to utter. *The enemy of my enemy is my friend.* For that reason, I pursed my lips and kept my counsel, rolling the dice of fate.

"Come", Kul shouted, and led the band off the well-trodden path into a ravine to the right.

He must have noticed my questioning glare, and for some inexplicable reason he succumbed to the urge to enlighten me. Mayhap, in the face of great danger any man yearns for allies, however unlikely. Or maybe it was just that he needed to calm himself by uttering words.

"The twelve tribes of the land of *Bazgun* have learned to live in peace", he said. "But the chieftains of the thirteenth tribe are unlike the others. The tyrants who hail from the land beyond the rising sun are a vicious breed. This will not rest until they have subjugated all in their path."

Chapter 22 – Oath

Judging by how hard they pushed the horses, it was evident that the Saragurs feared the Avars. By the time that the sun was high in the sky, the animals were exhausted, and Kul was forced to call a halt at a stream. While the men took care of their mounts, the four of us were unceremoniously bunched off to the side and tied to the grey stump of a long-dead tree at the edge of a hornbeam thicket.

Half an hour later, having rested and watered the horses, our captors made ready to depart. They were about to load us onto the pack animals when a dozen armoured horsemen crested a nearby rise - one of the many that defined the undulating grassland.

To their credit, the Saragurs did not panic. They knew that their horses were too weary to ride clear of the threat, so they reached for their strung bows and immediately released arrows at the advancing line of riders. But the heads and chests of the Avar horses were protected by iron scale and their riders encased in near-impenetrable lamellar armour – hundreds of tiny, overlapping iron plates that had been sewn onto a backing of soft leather. The armour extended to their knees and elbows, which were in turn protected by greaves and vambraces forged from iron plate. Lamellar iron helmets with thick nose guards, cheek plates, and mailed fringes prevented missiles from striking their faces and necks.

The attackers leaned forward to present the smallest possible targets, and rode low in their saddles, the black horse hair plumes of their conical helmets fluttering in the draft.

When thirty paces separated them from the Saragurs, the Avars lowered the hafts of their ten-feet-long lances. Three heartbeats later, a wall of horseflesh slammed into the *Kügels*, the armour-piercing iron tips slicing through the Saragurs' armour with astonishing ease, impaling chests, necks and skulls.

Not even one of the attackers were unhorsed when they struck the Saragur line. The Avar horsemen appeared to be glued to the backs of their mounts, and even the bone-jarring impacts did not so much as lift them from their saddles. Only then did I notice that the toes of their booted feet were supported by strange iron rings that hung from leather straps attached to their saddles.

At least ten of our captors fell to the lances of the attackers in the initial charge. I spied two empty Avar saddles and knew that the odds still favoured the defenders. Within moments the attackers discarded their lances and curved sabres found their way into their fists.

The *Kügels* released a last volley at the armoured horsemen in a desperate attempt to whittle down the foe's numbers before it came to close quarters. Then they drew their swords and battle-axes and the charge became a bloody melee.

A badly aimed shaft from a Saragur bow missed its target and arced high in the sky. I saw my doom falling from above. Straining at the tight bindings, I managed to duck, and the three-bladed arrowhead embedded in the wood just above my head.

Kursik was the first to regain his wits. "Our fate will be no different at the hands of these Avars", he said. "They are a vile breed who will use us for sport."

"I don't think they even know we're here", Beremud whispered.

The Avars and the Saragurs were battling to the death and, shaded by the thicket, none gave us any heed. I propped myself up, twisted my neck and managed to get my teeth onto the shaft of the arrow, wiggling it back and forth until it came free of the rotting wood.

For fear of dropping the arrow, I could not speak, but my friends divined my intentions.

I slid down the trunk as far as possible and used the razor edge of the whetted tip to saw through the bonds binding Beremud, who was standing on his toes so that I could reach. Notwithstanding the profanities he issued every time I drew blood, I eventually cut through the leather.

While Beremud untied us, I rubbed my bleeding wrists and stole a glance at the fight that was still raging. The Avars were getting the upper hand, raising themselves from their saddles by anchoring their feet in the iron rings and slashing down at their foes, who found themselves outnumbered.

We picked up the cut bindings and skulked into the underbrush. There was nowhere to run, and all that we could hope for was that the Avars would kill the Saragurs and return whence they came.

The gods answered our prayers. Within two hundred heartbeats it was all over, the ground littered with *Kügel* dead and dying.

One of the Avars, a noble, judging by the quality of his loose-fitting, embroidered robes protruding from underneath his armour, removed his helmet and passed it to an underling. The man's hair was black and shiny as a raven's, and hung loose to his shoulders. His cheeks carried no beard and his eyes were slanted like the Easterners whom I had seen in the City of Constantine.

Noticing the empty saddle belonging to one of his own, he swung down from his horse and went to kneel beside a prone form sprawled amongst the Saragur bodies. The injured warrior had taken a wound in the final onslaught and was bleeding profusely from a deep cut at the base of his neck where a blade had cleaved the flesh.

The injury to the prone man had a profound effect on the Avar noble, who lifted the dying man into his arms and pressed the warrior against his chest, wails of despair coming from his lips.

"Poor bloody bastard", Beremud growled from beside me. "He's certainly seen his last sunrise."

"Maybe it's a good thing", Kursik said and shrugged. "If their leader's so affected by his kin's death, he's bound to head home sooner."

"*Do not harden your heart and turn away from healing the needy*", I heard Jacob mutter from beside me. He spoke the words as if reciting an oath to the gods, and I immediately knew that no good would come of it. I turned to stop him from whatever he intended to do, but it was already too late.

I grabbed at Jacob's arm, but he plucked it away and stepped into the sunshine, his palms open and held out to the side.

"I wish to help the wounded warrior", he shouted in Greek while making his way towards the leader who was still on his knees, tending to the injured man.

I knew that there was little chance that the Eastern nomads would understand Greek. For all that it mattered, Jacob might as well have stormed towards them with a blade in his hand. Already the Avar warriors were jerking their mounts' heads around to deal with the new threat.

Feeling the tug of fate, I sprang to my feet and rushed to Jacob's side, while shouting in the tongue of the Sea of Grass, "This man is a healer. Allow him to tend to your injured."

The horsemen dug their heels into the sides of their mounts, roared what I assumed was a war cry, and thundered down on us, blades bared and lances horizontal.

But the noble with the Eastern features gained his feet and barked a command. Immediately the riders reined in, grounded their spears, and sheathed their blades.

All the while, Jacob, as if in a trance, never stopped walking toward his patient, still mumbling to himself. I kept to his side, making sure to keep my palms in the open.

The Avar noble made eye contact, laid down the dying man, and retreated a step. Then he drew his wicked blade.

My friend was none the wiser, but I knew what the gesture meant. If the man succumbed to his wounds, our lives would be forfeit as well.

The Jew kneeled beside the prone man and dabbed away the red welling from the deep cut before pulling the open wound this way and that. The injured man moaned in pain, and I noticed the Avar noble's knuckles whiten around the pommel of his sabre.

"Ask the savage if they have vinegar, honey, linen, a thin needle, and sinew thread", Jacob said, his eyes never leaving his patient. "And tell them to boil water and come help me."

I relayed his words the best I could and thought it wise to touch my hand to my forehead afterwards in a gesture of respect.

In response, the noble issued a string of commands. Soon Jacob was stitching inside the wound with the needle and sinew that he had cleaned with vinegar, while I soaked up the welling blood with linen rags. When he had stanched the bleeding, he closed the laceration with crude stitches, leaving a small opening for the pus to drain. Then he wiped the man's torso with water and vinegar and dripped boiling honey onto the wound before applying a bandage.

"*Put your trust in the Lord because it is He who wounds and He who heals*", Jacob muttered in Greek as he adroitly knotted the bandage into place.

"What did he say?" the Avar growled, the blade still clutched in his fist.

I gave him Jacob's words.

For ten heartbeats he regarded the Jew with emotionless eyes, then thrust his sword back into the sheath. "You are my captives", the Avar growled, before confirming my fears. "Your fate is tied to that of my brother's."

* * *

Without ceremony, the Avars floated the Saragur dead down the stream, then, on Jacob's insistence, pitched camp on the grass-covered bank. They did not truss us up, but four armed guards kept their eyes on us all the time.

We were seated around the cooking fire when Jacob ducked from the tent of the noble and made his way to the fireside.

"How is he?" Beremud asked, not that he cared for the life of the Avar, but because he knew what the consequences would be if the noble succumbed to his wounds.

Jacob shrugged in reply. "Not worse than earlier."

"Where did you learn your healing skills?" I asked in an attempt to change the subject.

"Twenty years ago, when Attila approached the Great City of Constantine and Isaurian soldiers repelled the attacks from the hastily repaired wall, my father was the chief imperial physician of Theodosius II", he said.

Leodis had told me that the emperor at that time forbade Jacob's people to serve the state, so I must have frowned.

"Laws do not apply to the emperor", he said with half a smile. "Especially when it concerns his health."

"In any event", he continued, "In those days I was an understudy to my father. I helped him to treat the terrible wounds of the never-ending stream of injured soldiers returning from the front. We saved many lives, but alas, the people of the city soon forgot what we had done. One night my father walked home from tending to a patient and he was attacked by a mob. They didn't kill him, but he was never the same thereafter."

He took a bite from a round of goat cheese and swallowed it down with a swig of water.

"That's when I decided to rather become a merchant", he said. "I felt that the people of the city had wronged us for no reason and I hardened my heart to their pleas."

Then Jacob's shoulders slumped. "But in truth, I had been unfaithful to our God, because, years before I had given my father, who was called Asaph, an oath – a promise that I swore before the God of my forefathers. It has haunted me ever since I left the city. Today, when I saw the man dying, I felt that I needed to be true to my oath."

Everyone has their demons and it was no different with Jacob.

Before we could offer a reply, the Avar nobleman appeared from the darkness. My first thought was that his brother had died and that he had come to claim our heads, but it was all but that.

The man looked at Jacob. "My brother is awake and he speaks", he said. "Come, you will assist me so that I may sacrifice to the God that you worship, healer. It is due to His intervention that my brother lives."

Chapter 23 – Baian

We remained encamped in the same place for another three days until it was evident that the injured nobleman would recover. Baian, who commanded the Avar warband, had taken a liking to our Jewish friend, which was something I noticed even before his brother's condition had improved.

"I have been given my freedom", he told us on the last evening we spent amongst the nomads.

"What about the rest of us?" Beremud asked, a frown furrowing his brow.

"Lord Baian wished to sell you as slaves", Jacob said. "But he has given me the choice of a reward of gold or your freedom."

"So what did you choose?" Beremud asked, his frown deepening.

"I remember Lord Abdarakos told me that one does not gain gold at the expense of a guest friend", Jacob replied.

Kursik, Beremud and I all issued sighs of relief. Although I had expected it, given Jacob's success in healing the brother of Baian, I knew only too well how fickle the upper classes could be.

Then Jacob passed me a purse heavy with coin, the smile still plastered on his face. "Because I value my friends above the gold, Lord Baian gave me the coin anyway. I have chosen to share it with you."

I inclined my head as a gesture of appreciation. I did not know whether my gold had perished when our ship was destroyed. A purse of gold would help us reach our destination.

"The horse lord has done more than that, he has extended the hand of friendship to me and my family", Jacob added. "We will be free to practice our religion without fear of persecution."

"The people of the Steppes sacrifice to many gods", Kursik said. "To them it makes no difference if there is one more."

Baian generously gifted us ten of the blue roan horses he had taken from the Saragurs, as well as three decent swords so that we could at least defend ourselves. In addition, two of his men accompanied us on our ride west toward the Deep River. They would be the ones who would guide Jacob on his return.

The lands we travelled through were sparsely populated as most of the people must have heard that the thirteenth tribe was creeping west. Thanks to the presence of our guides, we did not fear an attack from the Saragurs. Few tribes would risk antagonising the horde of the Avars.

The closer we came to our destination, the more a darkness settled on my shade. I wondered whether Atakam, Abdarakos, Mourdagos and the others would have survived the raging waters. And where would they be? Would they have returned north?

Kursik must have noticed my dark mood. "Do not concern yourself with the fate of the others", he said in passable Greek. "If they were taken by the river, it is the will of the gods. Do not dwell on it."

He turned to the Jew. "Isn't it so, Jacob?" the Hun asked.

In reply, Jacob nodded sagely. "Who are we to question the will of God?"

"Before our boat met its end", Beremud said, "I spoke with the guide. Beyond the seven rapids there is a ford in the river. Beyond the Ford of Vrar there is an island where men have paid obeisance to the gods since time immemorial. There we will sacrifice in the holy grove – either to thank the gods that they have spared our friends or to beseech them to accept our comrades' shades into the warrior hall that lies across the bridge of stars."

I tried to follow my friends' advice, but it proved to be easier said than done.

En route to the *Burichai*, we persuaded our Avar guides to stash their armour on the packhorses so that they would not be immediately recognisable. Interestingly, the warriors did not share Baian's Eastern looks, and when Kursik questioned them about it, they explained that they were originally from a smaller, less powerful tribe who had thrown in their fate with the mighty Avars.

Eventually we arrived on the banks of the Deep River, close to the place where our boat had capsized a week before. There was no sign of any debris as the forest-dwelling peasants would have scavenged anything days before. We travelled downstream until late afternoon when we reached the crossing Beremud had spoken of.

"By the gods!" Beremud exclaimed when we reined in. "It must be as wide as the arena in the hippodrome of the City of Constantine."

"I can't even shoot an arrow that far", Kursik added, his gaze fixed on the far bank.

Carefully we guided our horses into the shallows, but soon found that the bottom was sandy and not much deeper than a man's waist.

That night we made camp on the western bank, hidden amongst the trees. I did not sleep well, as every time I closed my eyes, I saw the bloated corpses of Abdarakos and Mourdagos floating in the shallows among the reeds.

Come morning, we said goodbye to Jacob and his two guides.

"You are welcome to join us on our journey to the City of Constantine", I said to him. "If I remember correctly, you wished to get into the pine tar trade."

"We may have our intentions", Jacob replied. "But it is God who decides. Thank you, Lord Ragnar, but the Lord has shown me that my path lies elsewhere."

"Then may your God protect you on your journey", I said, and touched my hand to my forehead.

With Jacob and the two guides gone, Kursik, Beremud and I struck camp and made our way south along a muddy track which afforded us a view of the water. By the time that the sun reached its zenith, the wide river had split in two, creating what seemed to be a large island in the centre. The narrowing of the river caused the current to strengthen, and it was clear that anyone who tried to swim the deep stretch of water would be death-doomed.

The channel between the island and the western bank was less than seventy paces across, and we soon spied a handful of boats drawn onto a narrow sandy beach on the far side.

"We should signal them", Beremud suggested.

The words had hardly left his lips when two men launched a skiff and started rowing towards us.

"It seems that they have seen us as well", Kursik said and put a string to his bow.

"Do you think they will attack us?" Beremud asked, perplexed that Kursik would fear peasants.

"No", the Hun replied. "But mayhap they will try to extort coin from us", he added, and tested the draw of his bow. "An arrow costs less than a gold coin."

The ferrymen rowed closer and started to back water when they were twenty paces from the bank. They shipped the oars, and while the peasant closest to us stood to speak, the other dropped a hollow stone anchor overboard.

"Greetings, lord", the ferryman said while casually leaning on an oar. He issued a leer that indicated that the Hun had accurately divined his intentions. Judging by his facial expression, I harboured no doubts that the peasant derived enormous satisfaction from being, what he believed, in a position of power.

"Just say the word, Ragnar", Kursik whispered from where he was concealed within the shadows.

"Lord, may I transport you across the river?" the man said.

"How much?" I asked.

"Two gold coins, lord", the man replied.

Behind me I heard a creak as Kursik drew the bowstring to his ear.

"So, what will it be, lord", the man said, leaning on his oar.

I was close to giving a sign to the Hun, but bit my lip. "One gold", I replied.

"Two golds, lord", the peasant countered, and we will give each of you two birds for the sacrifices."

I knew that a reasonable rate was two silvers including the birds, so I decided to increase the stakes. "Kursik, put your arrow into the oar."

I heard a slight creak, followed by a whoosh. Kursik's broad-headed arrow slammed into the centre of the haft of the oar with such force that the ferryman was thrown backwards. Was it not for the quick reaction of the other peasant, he would have pitched overboard.

When the boatman regained his feet, all signs of spitefulness had vanished. His face was distorted by an expression that could best be described as portraying unadulterated fear.

"Three silvers and your lives", I growled. "It is my final offer and will not stand for long."

"And… and a very generous one if you don't mind me saying so, lord", the man stammered, his face as white as a bleached tunic.

Unceremoniously he cut the anchor rope with a quivering hand so that he could take advantage of my proposal before it expired.

Chapter 24 – Birds (September 474 AD)

The boat was too small for the horses, so we relieved them of their saddles and tied their halters to the stern post so that we would not lose them in the current.

"How far to the place of offering?" I asked when we had ascended the far bank.

"Less than two miles, lord", the peasant replied.

"Come", I said. "We will lead the horses. They are too wet to ride."

For another silver the ferryman volunteered to carry the wicker cages that held the birds for the sacrifices. "It's best that you let me handle them, lord", he said while we followed a well-trodden path that led deeper into the woods. "Not that they're heavy or anything, lord, but the little critters are lice-ridden, lord. I'm not saying that you're scared of lice or anything like that, but these bird lice are worse than anything you've seen before."

He carried on and on in an attempt to ingratiate himself with us. Rather, it achieved the opposite.

Eventually, Beremud, who was walking three paces in front of the peasant, stopped dead in his tracks and spun around while he half-drew his Saragur blade from the scabbard. "One more word and I will gut you where you stand", the big man growled.

Beremud was not the kind of man who issued idle threats and I did not doubt that he would follow through on his words.

Fortunately, the ferryman had enough clarity of mind to realise this. He nodded, too afraid to issue the verbal affirmation that might bring on his demise.

With the peasant ceasing to be a distraction, I noticed a towering green giant that rose above the surrounding canopy.

"Is that the oak where the gods are appeased?" I asked our guide.

He stared back at me, his eyes wide with fear and confusion. Every few heartbeats he glanced at Beremud.

"Answer the lord or I will gut you", Beremud sneered.

"It is, lord", he replied and wiped at the pearls of sweat on his brow with the back of his hand.

As we drew closer to the holy grove, I was able to hear voices. "You did not tell us that others are here", I said to the peasant.

"I thought that they had gone already, lord", he whined. "I brought them here days ago. I swear it lord, I didn't know, lord."

Just then I heard a familiar voice, the words clearly discernible. "The gods are not content with the sacrifices", the man said. "We need to give them something more."

"What about the peasant who rows the skiff?" another voice suggested.

"It's worth a try", a third voice said. "What do we have to lose?"

I could not stop a smile from settling on my lips, and when I stole a glance at Kursik and Beremud, I noticed that they wore similar expressions.

The ferryman was the only one not smiling. With a yelp he cast the cages aside and scampered into the underwood while the birds fluttered into the trees. I paid the fool no heed and stepped into the clearing underneath the enormous oak. Atakam, Abdarakos, Mourdagos and Kauko were seated around a circle of ancient stones, no doubt an altar of sorts, where they had been making sacrifices, presumably for our safe return.

"Good news for the ferryman", I said, and embraced them one at a time.

"Maybe not", Atakam replied. "We will require a worthy sacrifice to give thanks to the gods."

* * *

That evening we camped near the sacred grove, gathered around a cooking fire.

When Kursik, Beremud and I had relayed our adventure, the others told us their tale.

"The river god took the three of you to the eastern bank, but the rest of us were spat out on the western shore", Atakam said. "It is because you were fated to go east."

"We lost three good men to the river", Abdarakos said. "Forever their spirits will roam the netherworld."

"Without Bogdan to guide us, we had no choice but to travel along the shore", Mourdagos explained. "For three days we walked south along the riverbank, like peasants, until we reached a small settlement. We could not find a large enough boat in the town so we had to purchase two smaller ones."

Abdarakos reached behind him and produced something from his baggage that brought a smile to my lips. "A man feels naked without his blade", he said as he passed each of us our favoured weapons. "Your bows and your armour are on the ships guarded by our warriors", he added to set our minds at ease.

* * *

It took four days to reach the mouth of the Deep River where its waters spill into the Dark Sea. On the banks of the estuary, we found a shipbuilder who practised his trade near the blackened ruins of a city that was once called Olbia.

It cost us our two river boats and almost half of our coin to obtain a sturdy ship. The boat bore little resemblance to the sleek *skeid* which we had been forced to abandon earlier on in our journey. This boat, that Mourdagos soon named 'cow', was built to carry cargo. Rather than oars, the ship was fitted with a mast and a lateen sail. We used most of our gold to purchase supplies, and found a ship's master who spoke Greek badly, but on the upside, was able to understand the tongue of the Sea of Grass. He swore by all his gods that he knew the coast like the back of his hand. He also swore that he was born in the City of Constantine, which, judging by his command of the Greek language, I suspected to be a lie.

For the best part of three weeks, we sailed south along the western shore of the Dark Sea, with a gentle breeze at our backs.

On the twentieth day after leaving the Deep River behind, we entered the Bosporus. Our Greek captain proved his worth and used the wind skilfully to negotiate the powerful current drawing us south.

When the sun was low in the sky, he leaned on the steering oar and the boat glided into the waterway north of the greatest city of the known world.

No sooner had we entered the Golden Horn, when we noticed the approach of a Roman warship. I had spent enough time in the City of Constantine to know their purpose.

"Let us show them who we are", I said to Beremud and Kursik.

By the time that the Roman patrol boat drew near, the three of us had donned the armour of the men who guard the emperor of the East. On my recommendation we remained inside the canvas canopy at the stern.

I felt a slight shudder as the timbers collided. Moments later I heard someone jump down onto our deck, followed by the sound of hobnailed boots, which I assumed belonged to the soldiers that escorted the administrator.

The Roman functionary had selected our boat as his practised eye had no doubt noticed that it was a ship from the barbarian lands to the north. "I am the *centenarian of the port* and wish to see your trade documents", I heard him say.

"We have no papers, Lord Centenarian", our Greek master replied. "We carry little cargo apart from passengers."

"I cannot allow you to enter these waters without the necessary documents", the Roman barked. "You leave me no choice but to confiscate the ship and its cargo in the name of the emperor."

I knew that the Roman would have little desire to confiscate a barbarian boat. What he really wanted was coin.

The words that followed came as no surprise. "Mayhap I can overlook the transgression for a small fee", the centenarian sighed.

I ducked from underneath the canvas with Kursik and Beremud following close behind. My bearded axe, engraved with the markings of the excubitors, was in my fist.

Although the port official was a powerful man in his own right, it was common knowledge that the excubitors had direct access to the emperor. A whispered word in the hallways of power was all it took to condemn a man to death. And the functionary knew it.

"Ah!", he exclaimed and clapped his hands together. "My apologies. I did not know that loyal guardsmen of our illustrious emperor were on board."

"No need to apologise, centenarian", I said and made sure to rotate the blade of my axe for effect. "May I have your name so that I can commend you to the one I serve?"

"Leonid Glycas", he said and moistened his lips with his tongue.

"Centenarian Glycas", I said, and gestured at the harbour on the southern side of the entrance to the Horn. "I am sure that my superiors will appreciate the gesture if you are able to arrange a berth in the Prosphorion, preferably close to the Gate of Eugenios."

A slight twitch settled at the corner of the centenarian's lips as the allocation of a favourable berth would mean that he would have to forego a large bribe from one of the merchant captains who would be willing to part with much coin to be close to the market.

The centenarian realised that he was cornered and inclined his head. "It is not only my duty, excubitor – it is my pleasure", he said and issued a fake smile.

I reciprocated.

"Welcome to the civilised world", I heard Beremud say while the functionary boarded the Roman galley.

Chapter 25 – Trust

Jacob had told me that when Emperor Leo realised that he had little time left on this side of the river, he appointed his young grandson, Leo II, as co-emperor. The child was the product of the marriage between his daughter, Ariadne, and Zeno the Isaurian.

Soon after, Leo I passed away, and the six-year-old boy became the de facto ruler of the Empire. Zeno wasted no time. He easily managed to convince the senate to appoint him as co-emperor to guide his son until the young Caesar would become old enough to rule on his own.

But the politics of the Eastern Empire was dynamic, and I did not even know whether Zeno was still Emperor or if Trokondas, my mentor, still lived.

For that reason, we remained on board our boat until it was dark. Once the sun had disappeared behind the western horizon, the harbour, that had been relatively quiet until then, became a hive of activity. No wagons were allowed inside the city during the day, so the merchants utilised the hours of darkness to transport their wares and produce to the vending places inside the great walls. The Prosphorion Harbour was closest to the market, which made the Eugenios gate the busiest, and therefore the hardest to police.

Few men could pass through the gates without being molested by the city watchmen. But we were kitted out in the full armour of the imperial guard, so the *vigiles* on duty did no more than incline their heads in greeting as we passed, followed by the normal whispers of envy.

Zeno had appointed Trokondas as count of the excubitors – a position that held much power. Befitting his newfound status, my mentor resided in a grand domus in the old city, just north of the palace complex. We found the gates of the residence attended by two burly Isaurians who we knew by name from our time in the guard. Still, they asked us to remain in the street until they had spoken with their commander.

Beremud cast his eyes over the sculptured marble façade of the palatial domus while we waited. "It looks like Zeno's taking really good care of Trokondas", he said. "But everything has a price, eh?"

"I hope he hasn't sold his soul in exchange for this prison made of coloured stones", Kursik said.

We heard the approaching footsteps of the guards.

"We will soon find out", I said.

* * *

Trokondas embraced me like a father would a prodigal son. Then he clasped arms with Kursik and Beremud in turn.

"Ragnar", he said, "I did not think it possible, but I believe that you have grown broader in the shoulders."

"Try pulling an oar for two months", I replied, and accepted a cup from a slave.

He bade us to take seats on couches arranged in a corner of the chamber, and dismissed the pouring servant with a wave of a hand.

"Thank you for answering my call", he said. "There is much to explain."

He wetted his throat with a swig of wine and took a seat on the couch across from us. "When I returned to the city, Zeno asked me to forgive him", Trokondas said. "And that is what I did."

I, on the contrary, had not forgiven Zeno the Isaurian, and his words caused the anger to rise like bile.

"How could you make peace with the man who deceived us? Do you forget that Zeno was the one who betrayed us?" I challenged my mentor. "Zeno encouraged me to kill Aspar, and when I did, he had us arrested and thrown into a cell."

Years before, I had killed Aspar the Goth in order to foil a plot to assassinate Emperor Leo. But that was only part of the story. I had also sworn to avenge the death of Leodis, who had been murdered on the instruction of the Goth lord.

Trokondas shrugged. "Zeno told me that Emperor Leo had plotted the demise of Aspar with the help of his daughter Ariadne. Zeno believes that you are the one who betrayed him, Ragnar. That is why he had you arrested."

Trokondas took a long swallow from his cup before he continued. "Zeno also said that you wished to kill Aspar to avenge the murder of your Greek friend, Leodis. He told me that he expressly forbade you to harm Aspar."

"Did Zeno speak the truth to me, Ragnar?" Trokondas asked, looking me straight in the eye.

I issued a sigh. "It is true that Zeno told me not to commit violence against the Goth lord on hallowed ground", I said. "But I am sure that he wished for me to kill Aspar. It was not what he said, but rather the way he said it."

"Zeno told me that Ariadne would call for me", I said, clutching at straws. "And she was the one who led us to the chamber where Leo was dining with Aspar."

"You could have simply arrested Aspar and his son when they threatened the emperor with violence", Trokondas replied. "Yet, you chose to kill them."

I realised the truth in Zeno's words, but I was not about to relent. "I swore an oath to avenge the murder of Leodis, who was like a father to me."

"How do you know that Aspar had a hand in Leodis's murder?" Trokondas asked.

"Because the killer kept the company of the Goth lord", I replied.

"Do you really think that thugs only answer to one master?" my mentor said.

I did not reply, as Trokondas had sown a seed of doubt in my mind. No longer was I certain that Aspar the Goth was the one who had ordered the death of Leodis.

"If you are so sure that Zeno can be trusted", Kursik said, "why have you called Ragnar to your side?"

It was Trokondas's turn to avert his eyes. "Because I am starting to doubt not only my own judgement, but by sanity as well", he growled, and chugged the remaining wine.

The big Isaurian rose from his seat and started to pace about the room. "My countrymen have always held me in high regard", he said. "After Asbadus and I returned to his side, Zeno's position was strengthened. That is one of the reasons why the senate was so eager to appoint him as co-emperor – because they believed that Zeno's appointment would secure the loyalty of the Isaurians."

I nodded, as his words made perfect sense.

Trokondas plonked down on the couch opposite us and rubbed his face with his hands. "But then Verina, the widow of Emperor Leo, came to see me in secret one night", he said. "She told me that Zeno is planning to murder his own child so that he can gain the throne for himself."

For a hundred heartbeats we were all too stunned to speak.

"What kind of a man would take a blade to his own child?" Beremud sneered.

Trokondas scoffed at the remark. "How many men have killed their brothers, fathers or sons to gain a kingship?" he said.

"Blood is only blood when it does not bar the path to the throne."

Trokondas was right, of course.

"How does Verina know this?" I asked.

"The dowager empress told me that her daughter, Ariadne, confided in her", he said. "The mother fears for the life of her child."

"The same Ariadne that led us through the maze of paths so that we could kill Aspar?" the Hun asked. "Is she to be trusted?"

Trokondas turned to face Kursik. "That is exactly the reason why I asked you to come", he said. "I am in need of friends who I can trust. The survival of a child and the future of the Empire depends on it."

Chapter 26 – Child (October 474 AD)

The City of Constantine. One week later.

I approached the gold-inlaid doors that provided access to the chambers of the boy emperor. Blocking my path were two hulking guards, resplendent in the shining armour of the excubitors.

The larger of the two men issued a grin. "*Scribones* Ragnar", Beremud said, his voice mocking. "Are you checking up on us?"

"It is better than spending the day drinking with Mourdagos and my grandsire", I replied with a scowl, and pressed an open palm to my still-throbbing temple.

"Like you did yesterday", Kursik replied.

"I only wished to ensure that they had settled down in the accommodations that Trokondas has arranged", I said. "But they insisted that I share a horn of ale. Eventually I lost count."

"They might as well drink because we will have to wait for spring to find a boat that will take us home", Kursik said.

"Besides, I can think of worse places to spend the winter", he added and touched a palm to the stone at his feet. "Even the floors are heated."

"Are we having roast beef or grilled boar tonight?" Beremud enquired with a grin.

"Both", I replied. "And, even better, I heard that Trokondas has instructed the *count of the sacred bounties* to restock the cellar in our barracks."

"When does our shift end?" Beremud asked, suddenly eager to return to our lodgings. "And will you join us for a cup before the evening meal?"

I sighed. "I am afraid that I have onerous tasks to attend to."

"Like what?" Beremud challenged.

I gestured at the ornate doors, indicating the room beyond. "Once I have announced the changing of the guard to the *superintendent of the imperial bedchamber*, I will have to assess the quality of the delivered wine. And I still need to find two volunteers willing to share the burden."

"Maybe we can rearrange our schedules to help a friend", Kursik suggested.

Just then we heard the approaching footfalls of the night shift relief. Six hulking Isaurians halted twenty paces down the hall, waiting for me to signal the change of the guard once I had announced it to the functionary who presided over the schedule of Leo II.

Thrice I banged the gold knocker against the silver backing plate and took a step back to allow the guard on the other side to slide the bolt and open the door.

I was ushered into the voluminous chamber that was tastefully decorated with gold-inlaid furniture crafted from exotic wood. Intricate mosaics depicting the ruler of the world's illustrious forebears decorated every inch of the marble walls. The travertine floors were covered with a scattering of lush, woven carpets that helped to spread the heat from the *hypocaust* beneath the stone. Strategically placed cast iron braziers, incense burners and beeswax lamps provided additional heat, light and a welcome ambience.

To the left of the chamber, Leo sat at a large table nibbling on a simple dish of steamed fish and white wheat bread – fare that would not disturb his fragile constitution.

"Greetings, illustrious Emperor. May your rule be without end", I stated in the way that was expected of me.

The boy took a sip from a jewel-inlaid chalice to clear the remaining morsels from his mouth before offering a reply. "Greetings, *scribones*", he said, and laid down a dainty sardine fork in his plate.

He took another swig and almost immediately started coughing, choking on the watered wine.

The imperial physician rushed to his side and worked feverishly to stuff pieces of bread into both Leo's ears to remedy the situation.

Once the coughing had ceased, the imperial chamberlain fixed me with a glare. "I know you answer only to the count of the excubitors, *scribones*", he said, "but I beg of you not to disturb our lord when he is taking repast."

I bowed my head in acknowledgement of his words and could not help but notice that a middle-aged woman was comforting Leo, who had by then broken into a sobbing fit. She gently stroked his hair and whispered into his ear. The child clung to her in a way that indicated that she was probably more than a mother to him than the absent Ariadne.

"The guard will now be changed", I announced to the superintendent.

"And such it will be noted in the records", he replied, his tone formal, and indicated with a nod to a scribe that the necessary entries should be made in the register.

* * *

Later the same evening, Kursik, Beremud and I were sampling the new batch of wine when a fellow officer of the guard walked into the room. Asbadus, also an Isaurian, had served Zeno for many years until he, too, was forced to flee when Zeno incarcerated us after the death of Aspar.

Asbadus, who had been as disillusioned as we were, had also made his peace with the co-emperor.

"I saw Patricius heading towards Verina's chambers on my way here", he said as I passed him a cup.

Beremud's eyes grew wide. "But we killed him and his father Aspar."

"Not that Patricius", Asbadus replied and waved away Beremud's words. "This Patricius is a high-standing noble who commands the *palace guard*."

The *palace guard* had for all intents and purposes been replaced by the excubitors. The unit, that was once reserved for elite warriors, had degenerated to parade-ground troops and entry into the ranks was secured by a bribe rather than earned by the sword.

"Do you think that the dowager empress has a thing for him?" Beremud asked, sampling another vintage.

"Even the imperial class is not above falling in love, eh?" I said conversationally.

Asbadus choked on his wine. "Women like her don't fall in love, Ragnar", the Isaurian sneered. "Everything the men and women of the imperial class do is aimed at accumulating more power. Not even coin matters to them, just power."

"Trokondas told me that she's a decent type", I countered.

"She's better than most", Asbadus agreed with a nod, "but make no mistake - she's still of the imperial class. Poor bloody Patricius. He doesn't know what he is getting himself into."

Palace gossip was a major part of life in the guard and I discarded Asbadus's words as just that – gossip.

I spent the remainder of the evening in the company of my friends. We refrained from speculating about the doings of the nobles and rather told Asbadus the story of our travels. As an officer of the guard, I still had to do my night rounds, so I made sure not to imbibe too many cups of wine.

When the other three retired to their rooms, I strolled along deserted corridors, my footsteps echoing off the stone. While passing underneath a portico that bordered an extensive garden, I heard the sound of a twig snapping from the shadows underneath a clump of manicured olive trees. I had been taught the ways of the forest and acted as if I had not heard the sound. At the end of the walkway, once I was certain that I was out of sight from whatever had caused the disturbance, I stepped off the path, into the darkness.

I took my dagger into my fist and carefully made my way back to the olive grove, moving silently like Kauko had taught me.

When I was ten paces from the place I had heard the twig snap, I crouched down and bided my time, waiting silently in the darkness for the prey to show itself.

"He did not hear us", a male voice whispered somewhere to my left. "The Isaurians are brutes, but they are not hunters like the Germani."

"Mayhap we should have remained inside", a woman said.

"The walls of the palace have ears", the man sneered softly. "What do you think Zeno would do if he finds out?"

"He will not dare to lay a hand on me", the woman replied.

"But he would have me killed", the man said, his tone flat.

"That is not what I meant, Patricius, my love", the woman replied. "You know I will protect you."

"Come", the man said. "We must get back before we are missed."

With impressive silence the two lovers made their way towards the lamplit portico.

Every hunter knows that impatience is the biggest enemy. For that reason, I remained as I was for at least a third part of an hour. Just as I slowly righted myself, I heard something move. In the darkness, someone or something passed by less than a pace away. It must have sensed a presence as it paused for a moment, but I remained as still as the marble statues lining the hallways. It was too dark to make out features, but the sweet aroma of sandalwood lingered in the air after the person had gone.

Chapter 27 – Power

"Did you see their faces?" Trokondas asked when I told him what had transpired the evening before.

"No, but the woman called the man Patricius", I said.

"There are rumours that Verina and Patricius are more than just acquaintances", Asbadus said. "It must have been the two of them."

"What would they be up to?" I asked.

Trokondas peered down the passage outside his office and closed the doors. Then he joined us on the couches and kept his voice down. "The imperial class has an insatiable appetite for power", he whispered, echoing Asbadus's words of the night before. "I would not be surprised if Verina is plotting against Zeno. Somehow, she has drawn Patricius into her scheme."

He paused for a moment to gather his thoughts.

"Yet, we cannot tell Zeno that Verina and Patricius are plotting against him if we do not know for sure."

"How will we discover the truth?" I asked.

"I have known Verina for years", Trokondas said. "Tomorrow I will go and confront her. Mayhap if she knows that we know she will stop her scheming."

I was the only other person who was aware of the fact that Trokondas shared a relationship of trust with the dowager empress. Many years before she had entrusted her infant son to the hulking Isaurian, who, after faking the child's death, had taken him to the countryside, far from the clutches of Aspar. I knew that, given this fact, Verina would not have Trokondas killed.

Trokondas's plan was sound, yet none of us could have anticipated the events that was about to unfold.

* * *

Less than an hour later, when the sun was about to rise, I made my way to the quarters that the boy emperor shared with his mother, Ariadne, to announce the change of the shift. The excubitors did not do duty inside the sacred bedchambers at night, although guards were stationed at the doors to respond to any threat and to make sure that no one entered without the explicit approval of the emperor or his mother.

Zeno's chambers were connected to that of Ariadne and Leo's by way of a passage with doors on each side. Those doors were unguarded to allow for discreet access.

I had not laid eyes on Zeno since my return to the city, as Asbadus had been assigned to the co-emperor's quarters. I dreaded coming face to face with the man who I believed had betrayed me, although I realised that it was inevitable.

A scream emanating from within the emperor's chambers split the silence when I was but twenty paces from the door. The two excubitors flanking the entrance did not hesitate. At the third strike of the axe the lock shattered and the gilded doors flew open. I was first inside.

Ariadne and the young emperor's minder were wrestling on the floor, engaged in a life and death struggle. The empress clutched an eating knife in her right hand and she was trying to bury the blade in the woman's heart. The minder, who must have been the stronger of the two, had closed her fist around Ariadne's wrist to keep the iron from piercing her chest. At that moment the servant woman gained the upper hand and rolled over on top of the empress, revealing a bleeding wound to the back.

It took less than a heartbeat for me to assess the situation.

I grabbed the minder by the arm and pulled her off the empress, causing her to slide along the polished marble floor.

"Call for the imperial physicians and the empress's lady servants. And send for the count", I shouted to the closest guard. Then I motioned to the injured servant. "And restrain her", I commanded the other excubitor.

I averted my eyes and extended my hand to Ariadne. "Are you injured, lady?" I asked.

But the empress ignored me and scampered over to where the boy emperor was still sound asleep.

She took the child into her arms and started to wail uncontrollably. It was then that I noticed that the boy's complexion was like that of a corpse. And then it dawned on me that the boy emperor was dead.

For sixty heartbeats Ariadne cradled Leo's limp, lifeless body in her arms before she gently laid him on the bed. Then she turned to the boy's minder, her face contorted in a feral sneer. "It was her, and it was Zeno who helped her", Ariadne screeched, and gestured to a small leather pouch on the marble floor and then to the door leading to Zeno's quarters that stood ajar. "I saw Zeno giving her the poison."

The minder face was contorted in shock and horror, tears streaming down her cheeks.

"Execute the murderer!" Ariadne screamed. It was clear that the instruction was meant for me.

Just then I heard running footfalls approach from along the corridor. Moments later, Trokondas and Asbadus arrived, followed by twelve excubitors.

"Kill the murderer of the emperor!" Ariadne screamed again.

In response, the emperor's minder reached around with her head and viciously bit the hand of the guard who was holding her. For a moment the excubitor relaxed his grip and the woman darted towards an open window and threw herself into oblivion.

I reacted half a heartbeat after the woman dashed and managed to get a hand on her shift as she leapt through the opening. For a moment she struggled, my hand firmly closed around a fistful of linen at the shoulder of the garment.

Her eyes met mine. "I loved the boy well, lord", she said. "Unlike his mother who is the spawn of the devil."

"Why take your own life when you have the chance to convince the emperor of your innocence?" I whispered through gritted teeth.

She issued a snicker. "The evil witch will have me put to the irons until I confess to a crime she committed. Then she will have me killed", she whispered. "No, lord, I am done for."

She relaxed her body and slipped out of the garment, plunging to her death on the grey stones of the courtyard far below.

I spied movement in the adjacent window. Ariadne was leaning out, her eyes fixed on the mangled corpse of the minder. I could have imagined it, but a hint of a smile played at the corners of the empress's lips.

* * *

Once things had settled down in the palace, Beremud, Kursik and I made our way to the accommodations that Trokondas had secured for the Heruli.

Word had travelled fast and already reached the ears of my grandsire.

"Zeno had the boy killed", Mourdagos said after he had heard the story. "Now he can rule on his own. Besides, you already know he is not to be trusted."

"What about the words of the boy's minder?" I countered.

"Have you ever heard a peasant confess crimes without being tortured?" Kursik said. "They will deny it until the last bit of skin is flayed from their flesh."

It was clear that the Hun had experience in these matters.

To my surprise, the erilar had not given his opinion. But when he eventually spoke, it was clear that his insight into games of power transcended the barbarian realms.

"Verina and Ariadne ruled through the boy", Abdarakos said. "Poor little bastard never had a chance."

When he had captured our attention, he took a long, slow swig from his cup. "When the Goth lord, Aspar, wielded the power in the city, the Isaurians and Leo's family were united against a common enemy. Now that the power of the Goths has been weakened by the death of Aspar, a war is raging between the Isaurians and the imperial family."

The erilar took another sip and issued a snort of derision. "What does it matter who killed the boy?" he said. "Zeno,

Ariadne and Verina are above the law. Blood will flow as a result of the boy's murder, but it will be the blood of innocents, not the blood of the guilty."

"What should we do?" I asked my grandsire.

"Support the side that Trokondas chooses", Abdarakos advised. "He is the one who made you who you are, Ragnar. Try to see beyond the machinations of the ones who seek power and stay true to your bonds of friendship."

* * *

"I have spoken to Zeno", Trokondas said when he summoned us later that afternoon. "And he denies that he had a hand in the demise of the boy."

"Do you believe him?" I asked.

"No", Trokondas growled. "Zeno stands to gain the most, now that his son is no more. I fear that he is the one who removed the last obstacle that stood between him and the Roman throne."

Trokondas chugged what remained in his jewelled chalice and hurled the heavy vessel against a wall covered with exquisite blue-veined marble, the impact shattering the stone. "Mayhap I have been blinded by all these shiny things", he growled.

His utterance made me think of the words that Kursik had spoken a few days before, so I stole a glance at the Hun, but his face was a mask of stone.

"What do you think, Ragnar?" Trokondas asked. "Do you believe that Zeno had the boy killed?"

I wished to tell my mentor that I believed that Ariadne had murdered her own blood, but I knew that the advice that Abdarakos had given me was sage.

"I care little for the machinations of the powerful", I replied. "My loyalty is yours to command, Trokondas, and so is my axe."

The Isaurian nodded, indicating his acceptance of my words.

"I will not be made a fool of twice", Trokondas said. "I will not support Zeno in this."

"He is the sole emperor now", I said. "And he wields much power."

"Verina and Ariadne enjoy the support of most of the people within the walls of this city", Trokondas countered. "And what worth is an emperor's power if it is not backed up by the blades of the excubitors?"

Chapter 28 – Zeno

Two weeks later.

A servant of the Church led the procession. Although it was near the middle hour of the day, he carried an ornate lantern to light the way ahead.

Beremud must have noticed my confusion. His woman followed the Christian God which made him somewhat of an expert on the religion of the Romans. "Maela told me that it is a symbol of the True Faith being the light in a world of darkness", he explained.

Acacius, the Patriarch of the Church, followed three steps behind. Like a standard bearer of the legions, he held aloft a magnificent jewelled gold cross studded with gemstones and mounted on a gilded shaft. Because of it being a funeral, his vestments were all white, except for the undyed woollen garment that rested on his shoulders like a broad scarf.

"In the murals, the Christian God always carries a lamb across his shoulders", Beremud whispered. "I guess that the priest wears that scarf because a live sheep won't sit still for long."

The Christian rituals seemed outlandish, but I guess all gods are fickle in their own way, so I kept my counsel.

Behind the head of the Church followed a dozen white-clad functionaries who rhythmically swung silver incense burners hanging from delicate chains. Sweet-smelling smoke rose to the heavens with the prayers of the countless thousands who lined the Imperial Way.

The body of the boy emperor followed the incense-burning clergy. Leo II's corpse had been placed inside a casket of solid gold that was carried upon a cart drawn by four pure white stallions.

Emperor Zeno trailed his son's coffin by ten paces. He was mounted on a large white warhorse with plaited mane and tail. The stallion's gold, silver and ivory trappings matched the gilded armour of the emperor and was contrasted by a striking purple cloak that hung from his shoulders onto the horse's rump.

Ariadne and Verina followed in on open coach drawn by black stallions. The mother and grandmother of the emperor both wore black robes studded with pearls and edged with black fur. Their faces were covered by dark silk veils to hide their tears from the common people.

"I wouldn't be surprised if that witch is smiling underneath her veil", Kursik, who marched abreast of me, said.

My gaze settled on the empress, whose body was racked by sobs. Verina's arm was around Ariadne's shoulders, seemingly whispering words of comfort into her ear.

Beremud, who walked at my other shoulder, was also studying the empress. "By the gods", he said. "I think the Hun is right. She's laughing."

"She is crying", I said with more conviction than I felt. "If she had killed Leo, she would by now have convinced herself that it was a sacrifice for the good of the Empire. Although", I added, "the prosperity of the Empire is closely aligned with the interests of the imperial class."

Kursik issued a grunt, which I took as a sign of the contempt he felt for the upper classes.

We walked on along the Imperial Way. Thousands upon thousands lined the colonnaded porticos on both sides of the broad roadway. As we passed the onlookers, we could hear a muted rumble - the collective prayers of the great multitude.

While the procession snaked through the crowded Forum of the Bull, the sounds of mourning became almost overwhelming, and I wondered why the boy emperor was so loved by the people. He had only ruled for a few months and never accomplished anything of significance. In my own mind I came to the conclusion that it was because of his tender age that the citizenry was so stricken with grief. And, maybe even more than that, because they had been denied the chance to be ruled by a man of noble blood. Now, they would be subject to the whims of an Isaurian – a barbarian.

We progressed at the pace of a snail, and it took a third part of an hour to reach the old wall where we turned right and headed up the hill. The column snaked past a great stone column topped by a gilded cross with marble statues of Constantine the Great, his wife and his sons guarding the base.

Eventually, after trudging along for another mile, the procession came to a halt near the summit of the hill, not far from the gates leading to the Church of the Holy Apostles.

"Who built this?" Kursik asked.

"Emperor Constantine", I said.

The more the Hun stared at the towering marble columns, bronze-clad roof and gold tracery covering the domes, the deeper his frown became. "Does the God of the Christians live here?" he asked.

"No", Beremud replied. "But they keep the emperors' bones in there so that the departed rulers can be honoured by the people long after their deaths."

"Then Constantine is a fool who has wasted his coin", Kursik said and shook his head. "His shade is long departed."

While Leo was taken to his final resting place, the excubitors formed a ring of iron around the building to ensure that none of the *head count* would disrupt the proceedings which were meant for clergy and nobles.

For hours we stood outside, while inside the church the sermon carried on interminably.

Beremud used the haft of his spear to wind a curious peasant who had approached too close for his liking. "Why in the name of the gods are they so keen to get inside?" he said, and gestured at the church, using his head. "I wouldn't go in even if they offered me a handful of coin", he added and casually struck another curious onlooker across the shoulders.

An hour before sunset, the last hymn was sung and the emperor emerged from the gilded doors. The clergy remained inside the church, no doubt to spend the night praying for the soul of the boy emperor.

On the signal of Trokondas, the excubitors formed up in an open square to escort the imperial family back to the Great Palace.

It was then when the trouble started.

We had just passed through the tetrapylon, halfway between the Forum of Theodosius and the Forum of Constantine, when a rotten apple struck Zeno's horse's rump. "Child murderer!" a male voice screamed.

A heartbeat later, another missile, this time an egg, splattered against the emperor's breastplate. "Isaurian scum!" a female voice shrieked. "Crawl back to your hovel, barbarian."

A street mob can be as dangerous as an army of enemy warriors, and my axe was in my fist even before the orders of Trokondas echoed off the walls of the shops bordering the porticoes. I glanced around. There was no sign of the pious, tear-streaked faces of mourners we had seen all morning. We were surrounded by hundreds, if not thousands, of angry men and women.

"Not so brave, now, eh?" a voice said from the crowd.

"They're used to killing children!" another answered.

A handful of manure came out of nowhere and sloshed against the side of my helmet, spattering my face.

From six feet away, a woman hurled a broken roof tile at me and I just managed to deflect it with my axe.

"Restrain yourselves", I shouted to the men under my command. "We are not facing the enemy."

And then the mob surged forward.

A man struck out with a butcher's knife. I blocked the feeble lunge with the haft of my axe and hit the peasant against the temple. Another used the distraction to slam a home-made cudgel into my helmet, causing me to lose my footing and stumble backwards.

I shook my head to clear my vision, which I regained just in time to shove a woman out of the way who was about to bash my face with a sturdy bronze skillet.

I heard a heavy impact, and from the corner of my eye I saw Beremud collapse, a large dent visible in his burnished helmet. Within a heartbeat three knife-wielding men pounced on his prone body. These were no mourners, but rather reminded me of the street scum who accosted defenceless men and women from their hiding places in dark alleys.

One of the men must have pierced Beremud's armour and the knife came away red.

But one can only poke a bear so many times.

A red-hot rage rose from deep within, and as I hefted my axe to come to my friend's rescue, a bellow escaped my lips. "Kill them all!" I heard myself shout, and took the head of Beremud's nearest assailant with a single cut. Using a backhanded swing, my axe head crushed the skull of the second. The third man staggered backwards, suddenly more interested in keeping his guts from spilling from his opened stomach than stabbing my friend.

Within moments I sent another ten peasants across the river, and heard screams as my comrades waded into the crowd. When the pressure subsided, I stole a glance to the side and noticed a line of piled-up corpses separating us from our assailants. Five heartbeats later, the attack turned into a stampede as the attackers lost all interest in spilling our blood.

When the last of the vermin had fled, at least two hundred trampled bodies littered the colonnade, adding to the carnage that the excubitors had wreaked upon the mob.

* * *

Trokondas bunched his fists at his sides in an effort to control his rage.

"Why in hades did you give the order?" he boomed. "Three hundred of the mob are dead."

I felt the blood of the khan boil in my veins and stood from the couch. I was as tall as the hulking Isaurian, but had become even broader in the shoulders than my mentor, my back slabbed with rock-hard muscle from months pulling at the oar.

"What would you have had me do?" I growled.

"You made a mistake, Ragnar", he said.

I took a step closer until my face was a handspan from his.

"Beremud's life hangs in the balance because of you", I hissed. "Should I have stood idly by while the rabble gutted him?"

Trokondas averted his eyes, issued a sigh, and slumped down on the couch. He reached for an amphora and filled two cups. "Sit, Ragnar", he said. "You are right, of course."

I was puzzled by the sudden change in the Isaurian. Somewhat deflated, I sat down opposite him and accepted the proffered wine with a nod.

"It was not supposed to happen this way", he said, and chugged the contents before refilling his cup.

Again, I felt the rage stir. "You had a hand in what happened today?" I asked.

"Yes and no", he admitted. "Verina and Ariadne are livid about the murder of the child", he said. "Surely you can understand that, Ragnar."

Trokondas had a point and I conceded with a nod.

"The men of the legions are not allowed to enter the city with their weapons", he continued. "Inside these walls, Zeno is most vulnerable. Only the excubitors stand between the will of the people and the might of the emperor."

"So you agreed to allow the mob to get their hands on Zeno", I said.

"Not to harm him, but to scare him", Trokondas replied. "Verina and Ariadne wish for him to flee the city."

"So that they can control the senate and grab the ultimate power", I said. "How does that give them vengeance for the murder of the boy?

"Vengeance is not always about spilling blood", he said. "Zeno values power more than he values life. The ultimate revenge would be to take the throne from him and hand it to someone close to Verina and Ariadne."

Suddenly I understood. "Someone like Patricius?" I asked.

Again, Trokondas averted his gaze.

And then my rage boiled over, but rather than reach for my blade I used my tongue.

"You are the father I never knew", I said to Trokondas as I stood. "But somehow you have been infected by the evil that dwells within these marble corridors. I will have no part in machinations that has already claimed the life of Leodis." Without having touched the contents of my cup, I slowly poured the dark wine onto the stone floor to draw the gaze of the gods. Then I took my axe from its sheath and laid my hand on the iron. "I give you my oath that I will aid you if you are in peril, but I will not help you to destroy a man I do not believe is guilty."

Then I thrust my weapon back into its sheath, turned my back on the man I loved like a father, and walked from the room.

"Wait!" he shouted.

I heeded his words and turned around to face him.

"You are like a son to me, Ragnar", he said. "Right or wrong, I have chosen my path."

Then he embraced me and when he finally released me and turned away there were tears in his eyes.

* * *

So preoccupied was I to dry my own eyes with a sleeve that I nearly bumped into Asbadus.

"I heard what happened to Beremud", he said. His face fell when he noticed the look on mine. "Gods, don't tell me he's dead."

I shook my head. "Trokondas and I have a, er… , difference of opinion", I said.

"About whether Zeno or Ariadne murdered the boy?" he whispered while glancing over his shoulder.

"Trokondas trusts Verina implicitly", he said, and took me by the elbow to lead me off the portico into the manicured garden. "She believes her daughter's version of the tale – what mother wouldn't?"

Again he glanced around to make sure none were listening. "If you ask me, that bitch Ariadne is to blame for everything. She was the one who got us into trouble the last time, eh?"

Chapter 29 – Gold (December 474 AD)

I spent almost every waking hour beside Beremud's bed.

On the fifth day after the incident, the big Goth opened his eyes. "I'm thirsty", he croaked.

I pressed a cup to his lips and he took a sip, which he proceeded to spit out in disgust.

"I want wine", he said, "not water."

Atakam, who sat on the other side of the bed, shrugged, indicating that he saw no reason to deny my friend's request.

I poured wine into a cup and watered in down by half before holding it to his lips.

He emptied the vessel with a few gulps.

"What happened?" he asked holding out his cup for more.

"During the riot, a peasant must have hurled a brick from a rooftop", I said. "It hit you against the helmet."

His eyes came to a rest on the pristine burnished helm suspended from a peg in the wall and a frown creased his brow. "Kursik had it fixed the next day", I explained.

"Isn't there anything to eat in this place?" he asked.

Atakam disappeared through the door and returned with a plate stacked with smoked pork. Beremud wasted no time and started to wolf down the meat.

"Slowly", the old shaman advised.

"I am eating slowly", he said and shovelled more into his mouth.

When he had emptied the plate, he washed the last mouthful down with a swig of watered wine. "When am I back on duty?" he said, as if he hadn't been close to death for almost a week. "I am keen to get even with the riffraff."

"We're not going back to the excubitors", I said. "I have honoured my oath to Trokondas. Now that you're better we will be leaving."

My big friend shrugged. "Whatever you say", he said. "But the *Burichai* must be frozen solid by now. How will we get back home?"

"Mourdagos suggested that we travel west along the Roman coast", I said. "By the time we reach Italia the snow would have melted in the passes and we can make our way back north."

"Have you forgotten?" he said. "We have no home anymore."

"Abdarakos will ask Ottoghar for warriors", I said. "The king owes the erilar a favour in return for installing him as the ruler of the Heruli."

"When are we leaving?" he asked.

I pursed my lips. "We have one small problem", I said. "We need to purchase supplies, but we have no gold."

* * *

The rain bucketed down in torrents, striking the clay tiles of the roof with such force that we were compelled to shout to be heard. I stood to add more charcoal to the cast-iron brazier and refilled my cup with heated, spiced wine, which I sampled before retaking my seat on the couch.

"Ask Trokondas for a purse of gold", Kursik suggested. "He's the one who asked us for help in the first place."

"We had words", I replied.

I knew that Trokondas would assist me if I asked, but I was young and too proud to crawl back to my mentor on my hands and knees, begging for coin.

"Just take what you need", Kauko suggested with a shrug. "My people do not know coin. They take with the blade."

"There are thousands of *vigiles* inside the city", I said, dismissing the wild man's words. "Enough to overwhelm us if we try to steal the supplies from the merchants in the docks."

"Could we not earn it?" Abdarakos asked. "We have forty of the fiercest warriors in middle earth. Surely there are men in need of protection in exchange for coin."

Just then there was a knock at the door.

I peered through the peephole and spied a hulking form whose features were obscured by a hooded sagum. "What is your business, stranger?" I said and my hand came to a rest on the hilt of my blade.

"For hades's sake, open the door Ragnar", a voice growled for underneath the hood.

I undid the latch and bade Asbadus to enter.

The burly Isaurian stepped inside, unclasped the oiled cloak, and hung it on a peg beside the door to allow the water to run off. "Thank the gods for this miserable weather", he said, and accepted a cup from Kursik before taking a seat on a couch.

"You speak like a dirt-eater, Isaurian", Mourdagos growled. "Only men who till the earth thank the gods for weather that coats a warrior's mail with rust."

Asbadus issued a sigh. "I'm no farmer", he growled. "But the rain keeps the rioters at bay. At least we get some sleep during a downpour."

The Isaurian's words deepened Mourdagos's frown.

Asbadus wetted his throat with a long gulp and wiped the droplets of red from his thick, black beard with the back of his hand. "Let me start from the beginning", he said.

"The excubitors were the brainchild of Emperor Leo. He wanted to command a force of fierce warriors to counter the power of Aspar and his Goths", he said. "The Isaurians are much like the Heruli. We follow the old ways and still believe that an oath is a sacred thing."

Both Mourdagos and Abdarakos issued nods.

"The excubitors care little for politics", he said. "They draw their blades when the emperor is in danger and take the heads of the culprits. That is what they get paid for."

Again he issued a sigh. "But things have changed. Trokondas blames Zeno for the death of the boy Leo. My friend has always remained loyal to Verina, who has managed to turn him against the emperor."

Asbadus took another swallow. "Trokondas wields much influence over the Isaurians. His shunning of the emperor has caused a division in our ranks. Only a handful of us still support Zeno, which has made our duties difficult to say the least."

I nodded, as I was aware of the violent riots that had become an almost daily occurrence. More than once large mobs have attempted to gain entry to the palace.

Asbadus pursed his lips and I noticed a twitch in the sinews of his jaw. "Yesterday, when the mob tried to get to Zeno, I lost two men", he growled. "Now we are down to forty-three excubitors. Next time we might not be able to hold them."

"What about the palace guard?" I asked.

The Isaurian issued a guffaw at my words. "They are only useful on parade, and besides, Patricius commands them."

"So you need the Herulian warriors to bolster your ranks?" I asked, divining the purpose of the Isaurian's visit.

Asbadus took a long draught from his cup, but I continued before he could reply.

"I do not wish to choose sides, Asbadus", I said. "Trokondas is like a father to me and you are like a brother. You cannot expect of me to openly support you, and besides, we are still guests of Trokondas who is paying for our upkeep here in the Isaurian quarters of the city."

A sly smile cracked Asbadus's bearded visage. "That is why I am not asking for your blades, Ragnar. All I am asking is that your warriors assist us to load sacks onto a ship."

Abdarakos issued a grunt to show his displeasure at the idea of the Heruli warriors performing manual labour. "Heruli are warriors, Isaurian, not mules."

"And what if I told you that the pouches will be filled with gold", he said. "Would that make a difference?"

It was Abdarakos's turn to grin. "For the right price, Mourdagos and I will lash Ragnar and Kursik to a cart", he said.

"Not a bad suggestion", the Isaurian conceded, "but the route I have in mind is not suited to wagons."

* * *

Kauko and I led our band of wolf warriors along a covered portico bordering an expansive garden. The excubitors had extinguished most of the lamps inside the walls of the palace, so we relied on the light of Mani and the senses of my feral friend.

Outside the walls we could hear the screams and shouts of the rioting mob baying for the blood of Zeno.

Eventually we arrived before the doors of a room situated underneath the great hall of the emperor. The walls of the chamber had been hewn from solid rock and the heavy doors were forged from iron. Many times I had stood guard in front of the armoured doors, wondering what incredible riches were inside.

Asbadus stepped from the shadows, which made all of us jump - all except Kauko, who must have picked up on the excubitor's scent.

Without a word the burly Isaurian lit an oil lamp and removed a gold chain from his neck, which held two large iron keys. He inserted them in the locks and, one at a time, the well-oiled mechanisms opened with a click as he turned the key.

With a grunt he heaved against the iron, and the heavy doors swung open.

"Come", he said, and led us into the room every thief in the Empire dreamed to enter.

The flickering light revealed a chamber forty paces long and as many wide. At first I believed that the room was empty, but Asbadus strolled deeper into the cavern and the weak light revealed a heap of hemp sacks crudely stacked in a corner. "Twelve thousand pounds of gold *solidi*", he said, which made every man who could understand Greek gasp in astonishment.

"More than a million coins", I mumbled.

Asbadus raised an eyebrow.

"A Greek taught me my numbers", I said, which earned me a nod from the Isaurian.

"Every man will be able to carry a hundred pounds, which means that we have to make three trips", I said.

Asbadus nodded.

"How far do we have to take the sacks?" I asked.

"To the harbour", he replied.

"Good", I said. "The Imperial Harbour isn't that far away."

"You won't be loading it into the emperor's galley", Asbadus said.

I narrowed my eyes. "So where will we be taking the gold?" I asked.

"You will load it onto your ship", he replied, his face a mask of stone.

Although the Prosphorion Harbour was less than a mile from the palace, it took the best part of an hour to make our way to the docks. Asbadus had spent many years in the guard and he knew his way around the network of tunnels that the emperor and his family used to move around the city away from the public eye.

We emerged into an abandoned alley nestled between two dilapidated warehouses near the quayside, and fell in with the throng of thralls and labourers carrying goods to and from the ships.

"I have to speak with Mourdagos and my grandsire", I said to Asbadus while we made our way back to the palace. "This is not a decision I can take on my own.

"When I came to see you yesterday, we still planned to load the imperial treasury onto the emperor's galley", he said. "But Zeno's spies informed him that plans are afoot to seize the galley soon after it leaves the harbour. If you help him in his hour of need, Zeno will never forget it, Ragnar."

"Where must the gold be taken?" I asked.

"East, to the Isaurian coast", he said.

"How will we know where to go?" I asked. "None of us know those shores."

"Zeno will send a man", he said, dismissing my concerns.

"I will meet you at our berth within the hour", I said and clasped arms with the Isaurian.

Leaving the others to continue their toil, I made my way to the Isaurian neighbourhood within the city walls. We soon arrived at the house where Abdarakos and Mourdagos were reclining on couches, sharing an amphora.

The two grizzled warriors listened to my words while they sipped wine from their cups, their expressions alternating between looks of amusement and glares of anger.

"Zeno is a sly bastard", Abdarakos said when I was through. "But he is no fool."

"His cunning is to be admired", Mourdagos added. "If we go along with his game, we can earn much gold."

"Go tell the emperor that we will do as he asks", Abdarakos concluded. "But it will cost him a thousand pounds in gold."

* * *

I arrived at the harbour while the Heruli warriors were stacking the second batch of coin into the hull.

Asbadus did not flinch when I mentioned the exorbitant sum that my grandsire demanded. "Zeno expected to pay more", he said. "He said that giving away one part in ten is better than losing it all."

There was one last thing I was uncertain about. "When should we depart?" I asked.

"Ten days after you learn that the emperor has fled the city", Asbadus replied.

Chapter 30 – Mob

Over the next days the riots increased both in frequency, intensity and the size of the crowds baying for the blood of the emperor.

Apart from instigating the mob, Verina and Ariadne had also managed to turn the generals commanding the armies of the East against Zeno. But the Eastern Empire had learned from the mistakes made in the West, and the men who wielded the military might did not wish to turn the streets of the City of Constantine into a bloodbath – they were content to withhold their support for the emperor, and sit idly by while the mob did their dirty work for them.

Although Mourdagos and Abdarakos had sworn their ringmen to secrecy, they knew that tongues plied with wine were not easy to guard. For that reason, they confined the warriors to their quarters. To appease the men, the erilar promised them each a purse of a hundred gold coins if they complied with his orders, and threatened them with certain death if they did not.

On the sixth day after our late night escapade, Beremud, Kursik and I strolled down to the market to collect the supplies that we had ordered for our journey.

"Have you heard?" the wine trader said while we counted out the coin.

"Heard what?" Beremud asked.

"The mob broke into the palace yesterday evening", he said. "Zeno and a handful of his excubitors fled through the Lion's Gate where they boarded an imperial galley." He leaned in closer like a man who wished to impart a secret. "They say that he emptied the whole of the imperial treasury – nearly eighty thousand pounds of gold."

"I thought the Empire's treasury had been empty ever since the failed war against the Vandals", I said.

The wine trader flicked his wrist in a dismissive manner. "That's what the wealthy wish you to believe", he said, "so that they can take more of the coin for themselves. Did you see the solid gold coffin they buried the boy in?"

Beremud nodded.

"How come they can afford a casket like that when there is no gold to go around?" he asked.

"Where is Zeno going?" I asked.

"Word is he is fleeing to the court of the Western Empire to gather an army to take back his throne", the wine trader replied.

* * *

Two days later, I was helping the oathsworn warriors load vats of drinking water into the hull of the ship when I spied Mourdagos strolling along the pier.

The big man jumped onto the deck with an agility that defied his age. "It's been announced in the Forum – the senate has appointed a new emperor."

"That's what we expected", I said. "Verina planned all along to have Patricius installed as emperor. Now that they've achieved what they wanted to achieve, the riots will end."

Mourdagos issued a grunt. "The senate raised Basiliscus, Verina's brother, to the purple, not Patricius."

I stared at Mourdagos with an open maw.

"Story is that Basiliscus knew about Verina's plan, so he went behind her back and bribed the senators to support his claim." Mourdagos gestured to where the gold was hidden underneath sacks of supplies. "I guess the new emperor needs the gold in our hull to pay the bribes, so it will be interesting to see what happens when he can't."

Involuntarily I thought of the person who had overheard Verina and Patricius when they were conspiring in the palace garden weeks before. In my own mind I came to the conclusion that it must have been the dowager empress's brother, Basiliscus.

"The conspirators have fallen out, so the leaders of the mob will not get the coin that they have been promised", I said. "The treasury is empty and the senators will not be receiving the bribes they are expecting."

Mourdagos's expression turned serious. "There will be hell to pay", he said. "Come. Let us speak with your grandfather and prepare to leave this nest of vipers before we burn along with it."

* * *

Abdarakos listened to the words of his brother-in-law.

"I do not claim to understand the scheming of the Romans", he said. "But I agree. We must leave the city while we still can. When evil men are disgruntled, there will be blood."

He chugged the contents of his cup and slammed the empty vessel onto the wood of the table. "We leave tonight", he said. "It matters not if the emperor's man arrives or not."

The erilar had hardly finished speaking when we heard faint shouts from outside.

We exchanged glances.

"It looks like there is trouble afoot", Mourdagos growled. "I will get the men to arm themselves."

Abdarakos nodded. "And tell them to leave anything behind that does not have a blade or a bowstring."

I walked to the window and looked down on the street from the elevated vantage point. Down below, hundreds of cudgel- and knife-bearing peasants were wreaking havoc. The angry mob plundered shops and assaulted unfortunate Isaurians who had not yet locked themselves in their houses.

Abdarakos stood behind me, looking over my shoulder at the scene playing out in the street. "They are nothing more than street scum - common thieves taking advantage of the situation", he said. "They will soon tire when there is nothing more to loot and they have drunk themselves senseless on stolen wine. We will leave in an hour when they have lost interest."

I nodded, as the words of my grandsire made sense.

But rather than for the crowds to diminish, more and more men joined the looters and plunderers as the sun set. Across the road from us, half a dozen rioters armed with woodcutter axes were bashing open a heavy door while others chanted, "Kill the Isaurian scum, kill the pagans".

We watched the robbers break down the door. Soon screams could be heard and the attackers emerged through the shattered doorway into the street, dragging eight or nine men, women and children behind them. One of the Isaurian men tried to stop a peasant from assaulting what must have been his wife or daughter and was savagely hacked to death by the axemen.

I exchanged glances with Abdarakos. "I was wrong", he growled. "This is not going to get better. For weeks I have stood at this window, watching street scum who believe themselves to be warriors. I lusted to wet my blade with the blood of those feeble men, but I knew that I had to restrain myself."

Just then we heard the first thuds as the axes of the mob struck the door of our *domus*.

I heard the rasp of his mighty blade sliding from the iron scabbard. "Come, Ragnar", he said. "The time for restraint has come to an end."

* * *

"Let me go first. I have a score to settle", Beremud growled, pushed his way past me, and broke into a run.

The hulking Goth raised his oversized axe and uttered a feral roar that drowned out the sound of blades striking the door further down the hallway.

The big man slammed into the door with such force that it tore the timber from the stone and fell outward, onto the axe men, crushing them in the process. He managed to keep his footing and stormed across the flattened door to get to the mob. His own axe moved like a scythe, the iron cutting down five, maybe six, of the looters before they regained their wits.

And then Kursik and I fell in beside our friend while forty heavily armed Heruli spilled from the doorway behind us.

The man who I had seen cut down the Isaurian ran at me, his axe raised above his head, ready to split me from head to groin – a strike to be expected of a gangster who had never trained in the way of the axe.

I waited until he had committed to the strike and stepped from the path of the blade. As his blade struck the cobbled stone of the street the keen edge of my iron bit into the vulnerable part at the base of his neck.

Another two came at me from the side – one peasant bearing a home-made cudgel, another a flaming torch. I swat the cudgel-bearer aside like one would a troublesome fly, my axe first crushing the club, then the bone of his skull.

I blocked the downward strike of the torch-bearer, who I assumed wished to set me on fire, and ripped the blade of my dagger across his throat.

Then I turned to the Isaurian women and children huddled against the wall. "Stay with us if you wish to survive this night", I said, and turned away from them to gut another fool.

* * *

Slowly the band of Heruli crawled along towards the harbour. In our wake, the gutters flowed red with the blood of the mob. Eventually we emerged from the Isaurian quarters into streets that were almost deserted.

"We need to make sure that whoever has arranged the looting is distracted", Mourdagos growled. "All we need now is for our ship to be searched."

Abdarakos took the torch he carried and stuffed it into a large pile of dry firewood stacked beside a building. "Then let us show them how the warriors of the Sea of Grass cleanse men of their evil deeds."

"Burn it all!" Mourdagos bellowed. "These evil creatures deserve what is coming to them."

In response the warriors following us hurled their torches into anything that seemed like it would catch fire.

Chapter 31 – Sagum

The ship was crowded with at least twenty Isaurian men, women and children who had thrown themselves at our mercy.

When all were aboard, Mourdagos gave me a signal and I untied the last of the mooring ropes from the post at the stern and threw it back onto the boat. As I was about to jump onto the deck, I noticed movement from the corner of my eye.

A man wearing a *sagum* stepped from the shadows of a nearby warehouse, his features obscured by a hood.

My hand went to the hilt of my dagger, but before it came to violence, I had a moment of epiphany. "Are you the emperor's man?" I growled, my hand still hovering near the blade.

"It depends who you regard as the emperor", the man replied.

It was a voice I would recognise anywhere.

"Lord", I said, and went down onto one knee.

Zeno waved me to my feet. "I am at your mercy, Ragnar", he said. "You could earn more than the gold that is already inside your ship by selling me to Basiliscus."

He paused for a moment.

"Or just slit my throat, dump me somewhere in the strait, and keep all the coin in your hull", he added as another alternative.

"I could if I wished", I replied. "But you already know that it is not our way. The Heruli do not shy away from spilling blood - we follow the old ways of honour. Come, Lord Emperor, you are welcome on our ship."

* * *

We allowed the boat to drift from the berth on the gentle current. While we were inexorably pulled towards the strait, I stood at the stern, looking back at the city where the massive walls of Theodosius were silhouetted against an orange hue.

"The fire will keep them occupied for a while", Abdarakos said.

"Is it your handiwork?" Zeno asked.

"Their evil deeds needed to be cleansed", Mourdagos explained.

It was clear that Zeno did not know what the big man was referring to.

"A mob attacked the Isaurian quarters earlier tonight", I said. "They dragged the people out onto the street. It was a massacre."

Although the emperor's features were concealed by the darkness, enough moonlight penetrated the thin clouds and I did not fail to notice the dark expression that settled on his face.

"They say that the Isaurians are no more than base barbarians", he growled. "When I return I will show them how right they are."

Zeno was no longer the emperor. He was a guest on the Heruli boat, and Abdarakos addressed him as such. "Why did you not go west with the imperial galley?" my grandsire asked Zeno. "Word on the street was that you had fled."

"An informant told me that the ones who conspired against me had prepared a fleet of galleys to intercept me somewhere south of the Propontis", Zeno said. "Asbadus volunteered to go in my stead. His orders are to lead the enemy galleys as far away from here as possible."

Abdarakos handed Zeno a wineskin to wet his throat.

The emperor took a swig and returned it with a grateful nod.

"Sooner or later my enemies will find out that I have taken the Empire's gold and fled east", he continued. "Basiliscus has always been a fool and always will be. He will send his legions into the hinterland of Isauria to destroy me. But it is they who will taste defeat. I will lure them into the mountains where my people will crush them."

Zeno was no fool and I knew that any who underestimated him did so at their own peril.

After Zeno's revelation, we were no longer concerned that the warships of the East Romans would be hunting us. For this reason, Mourdagos made the decision not to attempt to navigate the Bosphorus during the hours of darkness. Verina and her cronies believed that Zeno was heading west, and our boat would be able to sail east unmolested.

The happenings of the evening had exhausted all of us, and once Mourdagos found a secure place to anchor, we settled in for a cramped night on the deck.

It was then that Zeno sought me out.

I gestured for him to join me at the stern where a few of the warriors were still conversing in hushed tones.

"I have been told that you know the sacred symbols", he said.

"I am familiar with the way of the runes, lord", I confirmed.

"Tell me about them", he said.

"My people believe that every word that leaves our lips are powerful", I replied.

Zeno nodded his agreement, but I knew that he did not understand, not fully anyway.

"Lord", I said. "If a man allows his thoughts to dwell on one single thing, that which occupies his mind will influence his deeds, is it not?"

"Yes", he whispered.

"But the thoughts inside his head will not influence other men", I continued.

Again, he nodded.

"When a man speaks his thoughts, he gives power to them - the power to influence the deeds of others", I said. "Once a word escapes one's mouth it is forever and can never be taken back. The effect it has on the thoughts and deeds of others are like the ripples of a stone cast into a pond."

He stared back at me as if seeing me for the first time.

"The written word is even more powerful", I said. "Because it is able to reach not only the ears of men close enough to hear, but it can travel great distances, and it transcends time."

Zeno nodded slowly. He was beginning to comprehend.

"The runes are much different from the letters of the Greeks and the Romans. When one carves the god whispers, the ripples in the pond breach the divide between the world of man and the realm of the gods. So potent are the carvings that they draw the gaze of the Norns, and bend the will of those who determine our fate."

Zeno thought on my words for a span of heartbeats, then drew an ivory-hilted dagger which he held out to me. "Beseech the spinners of destiny to restore me to the Roman throne so that I might have my vengeance."

Under the light of a waxing moon, I carved the sacred symbols into the hilt of Zeno's blade. When I was done, I drew the iron edge across his palm, and rubbed his blood onto the runes to draw the gaze of the fate-changers.

Zeno fumbled under his cloak and produced a fat purse.

"Keep it", I said, and turned to go and find a place to lie.

"You have done me a great service, Ragnar", he said. "I wish to pay."

"Do not be concerned, lord", I replied. "The Norns will exact a price. You will pay, but not in gold."

* * *

Zeno guided us south through the Aegean while my grandsire, who rarely surrendered the steering oar, made sure that he kept the arid coast of Anatolia in his sights. Late in the afternoon on the fourth day of the journey, after crossing a stretch of open water, we arrived at the harbour city of Rhodos.

While Zeno accompanied Abdarakos and Mourdagos to the market in order to secure supplies, I seized the opportunity and joined the steady stream of pilgrims strolling up the hill to the temple complex. Kursik and Beremud accompanied me.

Many of the men and women wore the clothes of the Roman East and spoke in Greek, the official tongue of the Empire. From amongst the mass of people heading to and from the Acropolis, I also heard the language of the Scythians, the

Goths, the Germani and other tongues that sounded foreign to my ear.

As we approached the summit of the hill, Beremud gestured at two enormous stone pillars at least twenty-five feet tall. "What are those?" he asked.

"Look closer", I said.

"By the gods", the big man whispered. "It looks like two legs with bronze greaves."

"Maybe they wanted to build a statue of their god but they ran short of coin", Kursik ventured.

We entered what used to be the sanctuary of the sun god through a grand marble gate flanked by Christian priests. I imagined that the followers of the Christian faith had taken over the temple for their own gain after pagan worship had been outlawed in the Empire. I placed a gold coin in the urn provided for that purpose, which earned me a smile and a nod of approval from one of the holy men.

Beremud gasped in surprise as we exited onto an expansive open courtyard paved with white marble. The Goth's jaw dropped as he laid eyes on the fallen colossus.

I stole a glance at Kursik, who wore a very similar expression.

"The people of Rhodos built it long ago to honour the sun god, Helios, for giving them victory over the foe who besieged them", I explained.

"Who was the enemy?" Beremud asked.

"Demetrius, son of Antigonus, foremost general of the man-god Alexander", I replied.

Most warriors knew the names and reputations of the famous Macedonian conqueror and his generals who had subjugated most of the known world. Beremud pursed his lips. "Then the sun god must have helped them", he said. "It is good that they honoured him."

We reached the massive statue and took a few moments to comprehend its sheer bulk.

"Where did they get all this bronze?" Kursik asked. "I did not know that there was so much in all of the world."

"The Rhodians melted down the swords and spears of the defeated Macedonians", I said.

Kursik reverently placed a hand onto the corroded metal surface that was green with age. He glided his palm across the thick, sculpted bronze plate, closed his eyes, and inhaled audibly. I was sure that he somehow wished to drink in the essence of the Macedonian warriors long departed.

"Did it once stand erect?" the Hun asked after a while.

"Seven hundred years ago it fell down when the gods shook the earth", I said.

Beremud shuffled closer to where one of the gigantic hands of the statue had shattered the marble like a titan of old who had struck the earth in anger. The Goth reached out and wrapped his arms around a giant thumb but even he failed to clasp his hands together.

"Maela will never believe me", the big man said.

Chapter 32 – Rhodos (February 475 AD)

"Rhodos has long been part of the Empire", Zeno explained as we sailed around the edge of the breakwater of the ancient harbour. "A fleet of East Roman ships used to patrol these waters. The presence of our navy was the only thing that prevented the Cilicians to turn to piracy. It is in their blood – they cannot help themselves."

Zeno paused for a moment, thinking on his own words. "Much like banditry is in the blood of the Isaurians", he added with a wry smile.

"What happened to the Empire's ships?" Mourdagos asked.

"The fool Basiliscus lost six hundred of our *dromons* in his futile war with the Vandals", Zeno said. "He underestimated Geiseric, their wily old king."

"I thought you had made peace with Geiseric", Mourdagos said.

"I did", Zeno confirmed. "But I was forced to negotiate from a position of weakness thanks to Leo, who entrusted an idiot with the largest fleet the Romans have ever assembled. Due to the incompetence of the new emperor, these waters lie undefended."

"At least it works in your favour", Mourdagos reflected. "Now we can sail to Isauria without being accosted by Romans."

Zeno issued a curt nod to acknowledge the irony. It was clear that he resented Basiliscus, and he turned his face away to stare at the far horizon. "We will reach Xanthos before nightfall", he said. "From there, it will take us less than four days to reach Side." He did not wait for a reply, but went to speak with the Isaurian refugees who were crowded around the mast.

* * *

Kursik was the one who spotted the sails on the horizon.

"Friend or foe?" Mourdagos asked.

Zeno did not reply immediately but studied the distant ships intently, his lips pursed. "Why would ten Roman galleys sail in a group?" he mumbled to himself. "No, these are merchant ships that band together for protection."

Our ship was not as fast as a warship, but still we gained on the heavy transport vessels. By mid-afternoon we sailed past them, making sure to give them a wide berth.

"It is good that we overtook them", Zeno said while staring at the ships from where sailors eyed us warily. "Xanthos lies on the banks of the river with the same name, a few miles upstream of the mouth. These large vessels move even slower in the river and would have prevented us from reaching the city before nightfall."

Late afternoon, we sailed closer to the shore, scanning the coast for the mouth of the Xanthos.

By the time we noticed three Roman warships emerging from the river, it was too late to turn around and run.

"Maybe they will leave us alone", Beremud said hopefully.

He had hardly spoken the words when, as one, the trio of *dromons*, all single-banked, changed course and headed to intercept us.

"Twenty-two oars a side", Zeno said. "Apart from the rowers, who are also armed, there will be at least fifty soldiers on each ship." He turned to face Abdarakos. "There are too many. We will all perish if you choose to make a stand."

Zeno had no comprehension of the way of the Heruli. Death in battle ensured passage to a glorious afterlife and was no deterrent for the wolf warriors of the tribe. As expected, the erilar's hand moved to the hilt of his blade, but then he paused, and a sly smile appeared on his lips.

I cannot be sure, but I will always suspect that in that moment, the Norns heeded Zeno's pleas and altered our fates that were carved into the trunk of the Sacred Tree.

*** * ***

The rowers of the Roman *dromon* shipped their oars and the sleek warship glided in beside us. Within heartbeats the two ships were lashed together. On the deck of the *dromon*, their lower bodies protected by the board, fifty armoured Roman marines stood at the ready, shields hefted and spear-hafts grounded on the planking beneath their feet. From the corner of my eye, I noticed the other two galleys take up position on our far side.

The soldiers' ranks parted and an officer appeared at their centre. "Declare your cargo", he boomed in Greek.

There was little doubt that in the aftermath of the chaos that engulfed the City of Constantine, some of the navy commanders had turned to extortion and piracy to supplement their dwindling income.

I stepped forward. "In our hull we carry the treasury of the East Roman Empire", I said, and gestured to a dirty and dishevelled Zeno sitting atop bags filled with supplies. "And the deposed emperor himself has come along to guard his gold."

The lower jaw of the *komes*, the commander of the three warships, dropped and he stared back at me with a look of incredulity on his face.

Slowly his expression morphed into a frown. "Do not play games with me, barbarian", he growled. "I hold your life in the palm of my hand. Do you think I am a fool to believe that this dirty Isaurian slave is Emperor Zeno?"

The other officers surrounding the *komes* issued sycophantic snickers.

Emboldened by the support, the commander continued. "You may keep your pathetic cargo", he said. "But I am seizing the Isaurian slaves if you are unable to produce the necessary permits."

"Including the emperor", he added a heartbeat later, his teeth bared in a wolflike leer.

"Now that will be against the *treaty of perpetual peace* that your emperor has concluded with my grandsire, King Geiseric of the Vandals", I said and my hand went to the hilt of my blade.

The leer disappeared from the commander's face.

I had earlier donned the magnificent armour of Abdarakos, and the *komes* must have realised then that in the lands of the barbarians I was a man of consequence. "Who are you?" he asked.

"I am Gunthamund, son of Gento, prince of the Vandali", I replied.

"You bear the markings of the Heruli", he said, his eyes narrow with suspicion.

"My mother was a princess of the wolf warriors", I explained, trying my best to appear bored.

One of the *komes's* underlings, the captain of the *dromon*, leaned in closer and whispered words in Latin to his commander, assuming that I would not understand. "I suggest we burn the ship once we have killed them all. No one will ever know. We will keep the slaves and buy the men's silence by distributing the cargo amongst them."

The *komes* grunted his agreement.

"My father will avenge my death", I replied, my tone matter of fact.

"Your father is not here, savage", the captain, who had earlier suggested our murder, sneered from behind the *komes*.

"He and his fleet of galleys are much closer than you think", I replied in perfect Latin.

"Words will not help…", but the captain got no further, because the *komes* raised a palm and silenced the man with a glare before pointing to the horizon behind us where ten sails had become discernible.

An expression of panic settled on the captain's face and he whispered into his commander's ear – this time keeping his voice down.

Without another word, Roman blades severed the ropes binding the vessels and on the *komes's* command the three *dromons* powered away, heading south.

"He chose the best option", I said as the Roman warships disappeared over the horizon.

"Yet, it won't help him when I retake my rightful place as emperor", Zeno growled.

For a moment I wondered what the fate of the *komes* and captain would be if Zeno achieved his goal. In response to my own thoughts, I felt a shiver make its way down my spine.

* * *

Four days later we approached the lights of Side during the hours of darkness. Zeno stood beside Mourdagos, who had his fist on the steering oar.

"I don't like this", the big man growled. "Even a small reef will tear through this worm-infested hull."

"There are no rocks here", Zeno said. "Only sand."

The Herulian issued a suppressed grunt in reply.

Zeno guided us past the harbour lights and then instructed Mourdagos to steer the prow towards the land. A hundred heartbeats later, we heard the familiar hiss as the timber slid onto the fine sand of Pamphylia.

Kitted out in our full excubitor armour, Kursik, Beremud and I followed Zeno over the board. Without even hesitating a moment, he started to walk down the moonlit beach, heading east until we reached what appeared to be the mouth of a river.

"The water of the Melas River flows from the mountains of Isauria", Zeno said, emotion thick in his voice. Unable to contain himself, he reached down with a cupped palm, drank greedily, and pointed at the dark peaks silhouetted against the starry sky. "Up there in the Mountains of the Deer you will find the *Place of Fog* where the water rushes from the stone."

For long moments the emperor stared up at the faraway mountains, and there was no denying that he missed his home greatly. "The only way that my people can be free is if I grip the reins of the beast", he mumbled and strode on, following the bank of the river into the hinterland.

We continued on for half an hour until we reached a towering sweetgum that looked out of place amongst the underbrush. Zeno ran a palm over the bark and surprised me by cupping his hands together and hooting like a fish owl.

He must have noticed my surprise and turned to face me, the white of his teeth showing. "As a boy I took part in some casual banditry", he said. "In Isauria it is seen as sport."

Twenty heartbeats later, Zeno received a reply in the form of a call that sounded much like one of the winged creatures of the night. Not long after, a dark form stepped from the shadows into the moonlight.

Our hands went to our blades, but Zeno stopped us with a raised palm. "They are my men", he said, and embraced the dark figure in a bear hug.

* * *

While the Isaurians unloaded the pouches of gold from the hull, Zeno took me aside.

"I love Trokondas like a brother", he said. "And I know that he is like a father to you, Ragnar."

I nodded in reply.

"Verina, Leo the Thracian's wife, and my wife, Ariadne, has poisoned Trokondas and his brother, Illus, against me", he said.

He reached out and gripped my shoulder.

"Verina and her cronies will send Trokondas to hunt me because he is the only one who knows the mountains of Isauria as well as I do."

"Will you fight him?" I asked.

"No", he replied. "The East Romans will find great satisfaction upon hearing that the barbaric Isaurians are destroying each other. I will not take up the blade against Trokondas. Rather, I will try to convince him to join my cause."

He reached underneath his tunic and drew the ivory-hilted dagger from its sheath. "I believe that your carvings are working", he said, his fist tight around the rune-carved hilt. "I can feel it in my blood."

I extended my arm and Zeno gripped it in the way of the warrior. "Farewell, lord", I said. "May the gods grant you your wishes."

"Do you not want to join me?" Zeno asked. "You will be rewarded handsomely."

"I cannot cross blades with Trokondas, lord", I said.

Zeno nodded. "Where will you go?"

"We will go west, to Italia", I said. "There, Tribune Odovaker will help us. We have much gold to lure warriors to our cause."

Zeno raised an eyebrow. "And what cause may that be?"

"Revenge, lord", I replied.

Chapter 33 – Burden

I waded into the dark water, making my way towards the ship that lay at anchor forty paces from the shore.

"Ragnar!" Zeno called when I was about to pull myself up onto the deck of the ship.

I paused, splashed back into the sea, and walked to where Zeno stood in the same place, deep in thought.

He acknowledged me with an absentminded nod. The gods had blessed the Isaurian with a keen mind, but more than that, he possessed a talent for scheming that was unmatched.

For long he stared into the blackness. I had no doubt that he had concocted a plan of sorts. What concerned me was that I would be part of it.

"The Western Empire is weak", he said after another fifty heartbeats had passed. "They have all but lost Gaul to the Visigoths. Many other tribes are waiting in the wings, ready to feast on the remains of the once great Empire. Once the carcass is devoured, the chieftains will turn their gaze east, toward the City of Constantine. And the East is not ready to deal with their onslaught – not yet, anyway."

Again, he gazed into the night for a hundred heartbeats, his lips pursed.

"The Roman rulers of Italia are unable to hold back the tide of savages", he said. "I will not engineer Nepos's downfall, but if worst comes to worst, the East needs to ensure the safety of its borders. The time has come to hand the reins of the West to a barbarian warrior with a keen mind – a man who is feared and respected by the Goths and other tribes alike."

I must have smiled then.

"You know of such a man?" Zeno asked.

"I do, lord", I replied.

For long I spoke with the Isaurian who had ruled the East, and answered his many questions.

Eventually we clasped arms for the second time that evening.

When I reached the ship, Abdarakos leaned over the board and extended his hand, offering to help me gain the deck.

I shook my head. "We have to beach the ship again", I said.

A frown creased the erilar's brow. "You should have spoken to us first before offering our services to Zeno", he scolded me.

"I have done no such thing, grandfather", I replied. "We will sail West within the hour."

"Then why do we have to go ashore?" he asked.

"To load ten more bags of gold into the hull", I replied.

* * *

It was still dark when we heaved the ship back into the sea.

While a gentle wind silently took us into the night, I told Mourdagos, Abdarakos and Atakam all that was said between Zeno and me.

When I was through, Atakam gave me his thoughts. "It is good that you told us, but guard your tongue, even when you speak with your friends, Ragnar", the old shaman advised. "A powerful man entrusted great secrets to you, and placed a heavy burden upon your shoulders. If you tell your friends, you will force them to carry the same yoke. Some burdens are meant to be borne alone."

* * *

A fresh breeze arrived with the first yellow rays of the sun. The lateen sail billowed in the wind, pushing us across the grey water at the speed of a cantering horse.

Beremud, Kursik and I sat cross-legged near the mast while we broke our fast on salted fish and watered wine.

"It was good to see the last of the Isaurian rabble", Kursik said, struggling with a particularly resilient piece of herring.

"What did Zeno want?" Beremud asked while Kursik, having given up on defeating the herring, swallowed it down with a slurp of wine.

I heeded the sage words of the shaman. "Zeno wishes for the Western Empire to prosper", I replied, which was not a lie. "He believes that the Goths pose the biggest threat to the Eastern Empire", I added. "If the Western Empire falls to the Visigoths, Euric's warriors will soon attack the borders of the East. The East Romans are not ready to face the horde."

"How will you achieve that which Zeno wishes?" Beremud asked.

"We have to do very little", I said, and pointed at a pouch. "Apart from delivering a few bags of gold and a letter."

Kursik shrugged, which was his way of displaying his belief that the fates had long before decided our paths.

"Is Glycerius still emperor of the West?" Beremud asked offhandedly while picking his teeth with a fishbone.

I shook my head. "The old man Leo did not approve of Glycerius, so, before he died, he had Julius Nepos installed as emperor of the West", I said. "A few months ago, Nepos arrived in Rome with Leo's army at his back. Glycerius was forced to step down and join the Church of Rome."

"Due to Leo the Thracian's passing", I continued, "Nepos lost his support from the East. What is worse, he suffered defeats at the hands of the Visigoths as well as the Vandals, and was forced to cede huge tracts of land to both tribes. In Zeno's eyes, Nepos is just another in a long list of failed emperors."

"So, who's the scroll for?" Beremud asked.

"It is addressed to Emperor Nepos", I said.

What I failed to tell my friends was that the pouch contained two scrolls. One of which I was supposed to deliver to Nepos, the other to the man whom Zeno favoured as the ruler of Italia, the one who would shield the East from the onslaught of the tribes.

* * *

We kept the prow pointing west and followed the coast until we reached the coastal town of Attaleia.

Apart from fresh water and food, we were also in dire need of the services of a navigator as we had said goodbye to Zeno who had guided us across the Aegean until then. While Mourdagos went to the market in Attaleia, Abdarakos and I visited the drinking establishments near the docks. The owner of the third *popina*, a man called John, knew of a helmsman who, to use his words, had a rather urgent requirement to leave the city. According to him, the oldster, who was a man of sober habits, had fallen foul of the local government – why, he did not know.

Abdarakos shrugged at the words of the tavern owner. "We have no understanding of the laws of the Greeks", he said. "As long as the man is a good navigator."

"He is the very best", the barman said, looked around to make sure no one was listening, and lowered his voice. "Even though he is a pagan."

We made our way down the street, following the directions that we had been given. As we arrived at the small house of the navigator, we were confronted by two city guardsmen flanking the open door. From inside the *domus* we heard screams and shouts in a language that sounded foreign to our ears.

"Off with you, outlanders", one of the guards growled and waved a hand in a sign of dismissal. "Interfering in the business of the bishop is a capital offence."

"Is a priest the headman of the town?" Abdarakos asked, not in the least intimidated by the guardsman.

The man, who had had time to study us, must have come to the conclusion that the preferred option would be for us to leave at our own accord. "The bishop and the patrons lead the council", he explained reluctantly.

Another scream came from inside.

"And they enforce the laws of our dear and beloved emperor", he added by way of explanation.

"What has this man done?" I asked.

"He is a pagan", the other guard whispered, as if saying the words out loud would doom him to the same fate as the unfortunate inside.

"And", the first guard added, "he is accused of slaughtering a goat and sacrificing it to Set, the terrible god of the Aegyptians."

Most citizens of Attaleia would have been appalled at the revelation, but Abdarakos stood unblinking, clearly confused in terms of what all the fuss was about.

Just then, two more burly guards emerged into the street from inside the house. Between them they dragged a writhing figure – an oldster with dark olive skin and silver hair.

"What is Set the god of?" Abdarakos asked the nearest guardsman.

And then one of the watchmen who were dragging the oldster along made a fatal mistake. He reached out to shove Abdarakos out of his way.

With practised ease, the erilar grabbed the guard's wrist in a grip of iron and twisted his arm so that he was forced to bend over. In one fluent motion my grandsire drew his dagger and rammed the blade into the back of the man's neck.

Before the other guardsman could respond, the flat of my axe crushed his skull and he crumpled to the ground.

The third watchman drew his own dagger and slashed at Abdarakos, who took the pathetic strike on his armour, grabbed the man by the neck, and slammed his forehead into his nose. The erilar did not relinquish his grip, but pulled the dazed watchman in close and opened his neck with a blade.

The last man staggered backward in an attempt to escape the slaughter. In his haste he tripped and fell down, but managed to right himself. As he turned to run, my axe whirred through the air and bit deep into his spine.

"Violence", I said while I pried the blade of my bearded axe from the corpse.

My grandsire gave me a quizzical look.

"Set is the Aegyptian god of violence", I said, and bent down to wipe the blood from the iron.

* * *

"The bishop is taking my house, lord, he is", the old man wept, "and I have been condemned to spend the rest of my days labouring in the mines."

"For slaughtering a goat?" I asked.

"I am a lay priest, lord", the oldster said while he wiped his eyes with a blood-stained sleeve. "I perform rites for people who still follow the old faith of the land that gave me life."

"What is your name?" Abdarakos asked.

"Attalus, lord", he replied.

"It sounds Greek to me", I said.

"Many seasons ago, when I left Alexandria to come to these shores, I was called Etamun, lord", he said, and gave us a gap-toothed smile. "Because I am a gift from the sun god."

"Come, Attalus", the erilar growled and presented the oldster with a gold coin. "You will be our navigator for we wish to sail to the lands of Italia. You will earn twenty more coins if you know the sea as well as John, the owner of the *popina* by the docks, claims. With that much gold, you will be able to buy a house somewhere in Italia."

"And if I disappoint you, lord?" Attalus asked, suddenly concerned.

"If you are not what you say, then you will curse yourself that you have not gone to the mines, for I will flay you alive and cast you into the sea", Abdarakos replied and slapped the Aegyptian's back.

* * *

Attalus turned out to be a gift from the gods. Once Abdarakos and Mourdagos were convinced of his skill, they allowed him to take us across the open water rather than hug the coast - a decision that drastically shortened our voyage.

Only once, near the end of our journey, did the weathered old sailor give us cause to doubt him. Although the sea was calm and the wind mild, he insisted we remain at anchor in the Greek harbour of Tainaron when we were about to attempt the six-day long crossing of the Ionian Sea to Rhegium in Italia.

We were anxious to reach our destination, but heeded the oldster's advice. After enduring three long days of boredom, a massive spring storm arrived from the south, and we were forced to pull the ship high up onto the beach out of reach of the violent waves.

Two days later, we set off from Tainaron.

Our hull was filled with gold, and the sea as flat as a bronze mirror. The pleasant weather and the coin lulled us into a false sense of security as we were about to sail right into the heart of a storm that the world would remember for centuries to come.

Chapter 34 – Italia (March 475 AD)

I was resplendent in the iron and boiled leather armour of the famed guards of the Eastern emperor, but it was the scroll bearing the seal of Zeno that secured the private audience with Julius Nepos, the emperor of the West.

I entered the room through grand double doors, went down onto one knee, and presented the missive.

A secretary rushed to retrieve the scroll from my outstretched palms, unrolled it, and held the document in such a manner that the emperor was able to read it without soiling his hands or having to relinquish his jewelled chalice.

Within the space of three heartbeats, the ruler of the West's complexion resembled the red stones set in his gold drinking vessel. With a flick of a wrist, he dismissed the slaves, servants, secretaries and chamberlains, who scurried into the hall beyond the doorway. Only half a dozen imperial guards remained to ensure that the emperor would be safe from harm.

Julius Nepos rose from his throne and cast the scroll into a corner. "Zeno has the audacity to believe that he can tell me, the emperor, what to do", he hissed. "He is nothing more than a barbarian cowering in the Anatolian hills. I have the support of my cousin, Basiliscus. So, you see, I do not need the favour of a barbarian, especially an Isaurian brigand."

"Zeno cautions me not to trust General Orestes", he chuckled. "But Orestes is an honourable man who has sworn before God that he will never take the throne of Rome. Zeno has not only lost his rule but he has become paranoid as well."

Having vented his rage, Nepos retook his seat. "Tell your master that I do not need his patronage", he growled. "Now remove yourself from my presence, excubitor, before I decide to send your head to your lord instead."

"I will do as you command, Lord Emperor", I lied in Greek, and backpedaled from the chamber.

* * *

"Zeno told me that the emperor is a man full of self-importance", I said to Abdarakos while the small imperial transport glided along a canal, headed for Portus, Rome's massive harbour on the Tiber. "He also said that Nepos would not heed his words. The emperor favours a general called

Orestes, a Roman who served Attila. In his letter, Zeno warned him about Orestes's ambition."

At the mention of the name, a sneer settled on the face of the Abdarakos, who once commanded the armies of the great khan. "Orestes, son of Tatulus, is a man with an insatiable lust for power", the erilar growled. "He is a Roman patrician who betrayed his own people. Only his fear of Attila kept him in check. When the great khan passed, he abandoned the Huns and scurried back to Italia."

My grandsire drew a deep breath to calm himself.

"Orestes knows the ways of the tribesmen who fight in the armies of Rome", Abdarakos continued. "And he does not fear Nepos. If the emperor appoints Orestes as the master of the Western armies, he will use his newfound power to claim the throne for himself."

"Emperor Nepos told me that Orestes had sworn fealty to him before the Christian God", I said.

Abdarakos chuckled as if I had told him a jest. "I know that Orestes, like his father, sacrifices to the old gods. He would think nothing of breaking an oath he had given to the God of Rome."

"Then we had better get to Ravenna quickly", I said. "I need to deliver another scroll."

* * *

"Two weeks, lord", Attalus said. "If the wind holds."

"It will take only six days to ride to Ravenna", Kursik said. "And we have no time to waste."

I suspected that getting back into the saddle was the main reason the Hun preferred travelling on horseback.

"We have no papers", Abdarakos said. "And if the emperor gets wind that we have not returned East, it will not go well for us."

My grandsire clasped Kursik's armoured shoulder. "When we reach Aquileia I will purchase you the best horse money can buy."

"I wish for a Berber mare", the Hun replied, immediately placated.

"A Berber horse it will be", the erilar confirmed and followed Kursik onto the deck.

* * *

Fourteen days later we sailed past the stone-built breakwater of Classe, Ravenna's harbour town, and entered the channel giving access to the estuary. Many years earlier, even before the Romans ruled all of Italia, ancient tribes had settled on the islands in the lagoon. These patches of dry land were surrounded by swamps and salt marshes, which served as natural defences. It was for this reason that more than seventy years before, the capital of the Empire had been moved to Ravenna. Still, the emperor of the time had thought it best to improve the defences and he had ordered the construction of massive stone walls, thirty feet high and eight feet thick. Since then, successive rulers had added towers, bridges and gates, rendering the capital a near-impregnable fortress.

On exiting the waterway, Abdarakos did not turn right towards the city, but leaned on the steering oar. The vessel rounded the headland and swerved to the left where many smaller merchant ships lay at anchor at the harbour of Classe.

Attalus stared up at the towering stone walls abutting the concrete quayside. "When I was a young man, an oldster told me that he had visited Classe when he was a ship's boy. In those days Roman warships filled every berth."

Not a single Roman galley could be seen, which made our navigator's claim sound preposterous.

"I have heard it as well", Mourdagos confirmed. "Geiseric is to blame. Once the Vandals had taken control of the Roman provinces in Africa, they started raiding the coast of Italia and Dalmatia. All the Roman warships that used to be stationed at this harbour have either been taken by Geiseric's pirates, or they lie at the bottom of the Middle Sea."

I noticed a group of Roman soldiers marching along the quayside.

"The barracks that used to house the Roman marines now serve as accommodation for the *foederati*", Abdarakos said when he noticed the men approach. "These warriors will know where we can find Ottoghar."

"Who commands this ship?" one of the soldiers boomed as they came to a halt. I did not fail to notice that the warrior who spoke bore the circular, blue-green markings of the Heruli.

Abdarakos pushed through his oathsworn and confronted the man on the quayside. "I do", he replied, and his hand came to rest on the hilt of his blade.

"Forgive me, lord", the warrior on the quayside said, retreated a step to show his respect, and inclined his head to the man who had commanded the horde of the Heruli.

"We come to speak with Prince Ottoghar", Abdarakos said. "I heard that he is within these Roman walls."

* * *

Abdarakos was the one who had coerced the Scirii prince to become the leader of the Heruli. That did not stop my grandsire to go down onto one knee when he stepped into the quarters of Ottoghar. I followed suit.

Flavius Odovaker was studying a missive while pacing around the spacious chamber, his back turned towards the door. At the same time, he was dictating a letter in Latin. In a nearby corner, a scribe sat behind a desk, scribbling feverishly in an attempt to keep up with the barbarian commander. "… the warriors are not blind", Odovaker said. "The empire pleads poverty as the reason why the stipends of my men are in arrears, but the emperor is spending thousands of pounds of gold on …"

"Legate, you have visitors", the guard at the door said.

Odovaker, having stopped mid-sentence, failed to turn around. "My orders were not to be disturbed, centurion", he snapped.

"We have come to pay obeisance to our king", Abdarakos growled in the tongue of the Heruli.

Odovaker spun around, his frown immediately giving way to a broad smile.

The hulking overlord of the Heruli waved us to our feet. "In the lands of Rome I am no king. Here, I am Legate Odovaker, commander of the barbarian *foederati* of all of Italia", he said, and embraced us in turn.

Then his frown returned. "Many moons ago, news arrived from the north that you had been driven from the distant lands of the Svear", Odovaker said. "I expected you to come south, to ask for spears to help you regain your lands. When you did not arrive, I thought you dead."

"Without the favour of the gods we would surely have perished", I replied. "But it seems that we are not the only ones with problems."

Odovaker nodded, and indicated to a servant to pour wine before waving all of the attendants from the room.

"These are troubled times", he said as we took seats on the couches arrayed in a corner. "Since the emperor made peace with Euric of the Visigoth, the treasury is all but empty and Rome has reneged on the agreement with my men. My warriors have not received coin for three months, while it is no secret that Emperor Nepos holds great feasts where he lavishes his patrician guests with gifts of silver and gold."

Odovaker took a long swig to wet his throat.

"Nepos lost the war against the Visigoths and now he has to bribe Euric to prevent him from sending his armies into Italia." Odovaker's own words caused the anger to stir inside him. "The Greek entrusts the command of his armies to fools", he sneered. "And the *foederati* soldiers pay with their lives. I am tired of the incompetence and long for the days when Ricimer, the barbarian who learned at the feet of the great Flavius Aetius, used to be the master of soldiers. Ricimer knew the ways of war, and under his banner we crushed the enemies of

Rome on the field of battle. He cared little that the glory accrued to puppet emperors."

"Since Ricimer's death, the West has been on a path of destruction", he concluded and chugged what remained in his cup.

"Rome needs a new Ricimer", I said. "A man of barbarian blood, who understands the art of war and commands the respect of the *foederati* warriors."

Odovaker narrowed his eyes. "Ricimer came to power because he had the patronage of a powerful man and the support of the Roman senate."

"That much is true", I said. "But as long as the people are made to believe that the master of soldiers governs on behalf of a Roman emperor, a patrician of noble birth, they will embrace him. They do not wish to be ruled by a barbarian."

"The Romans are like sheep", Abdarakos mused. "They will gladly follow one of their own to certain death over the edge of a cliff rather than allow a wolf to lead them to green pastures and prosperity."

Odovaker and I both nodded because we were familiar with sheep and their tendency to follow their own kind, even to slaughter.

I produced the scroll bearing Zeno's seal from underneath my tunic and presented it to the barbarian general. "What if you had the patronage of the Eastern Emperor?" I asked. "Then you could be the one who takes Ricimer's place – the one who holds the Goths at bay."

Odovaker read the words that Zeno had penned weeks before. When he was done, he read it again. "It is a tempting offer", he said, and laid down the scroll beside him on the couch.

"But I will need the support of the senate to become the master of soldiers", Odovaker said. "It is an honour that they will only bestow on me if the legitimate emperor of the East is my patron. Zeno has been reduced to a fugitive who is being hunted by his own people."

"Zeno suggested that you garner the support of the senate while he addresses the minor issue of retaking the throne", I replied.

"And how am I supposed to do that?" he asked, issuing a guffaw. "In order to win the support of the city fathers I would need much coin."

A knock at the door interrupted us. Moments later, the door opened a crack and the face of the duty centurion appeared.

"There are a dozen Heruli warriors who seek an audience", he said.

Odovaker raised an eyebrow but deferred to Abdarakos, who grunted his assent.

One by one the men entered and dumped their heavy bags in the middle of the floor before leaving the way they had come.

I took a step towards the pouches, bared my dagger, and drew the blade across a woven bag, causing gold *solidi* to spill onto the floor. "Will twelve hundred pounds of gold be enough to purchase their favour?" I asked.

Odovaker's gaze remained fixed on the coin. "Probably not", he said with a grin, "but it is worth a try."

Chapter 35 – Arrangement

That evening, Abdarakos, Mourdagos and I dined with Legate Odovaker. My friends, Atakam, and the oathsworn warriors remained on board our ship to guard the thousand pounds of gold that still remained in the hull – our fee for transporting Zeno and the imperial treasure of the East to the coast of Isauria.

The Scirii Prince was a king in name but a soldier at heart, so we were served simple fare – spitted pork and freshly baked loaves of barley bread.

"It will take time to garner support within the senate", Odovaker said, sliced a sliver of half-raw meat from a joint, and popped it into his mouth.

"There is another problem", he said when he was done chewing. "Two weeks ago, while he visited Rome, Nepos appointed Orestes as the master of soldiers, the man who commands the armies of the Western Empire."

"Zeno advised Emperor Nepos not to", I said. "He must have appointed Orestes out of spitefulness."

"Orestes is a dangerous, unscrupulous man", Odovaker replied. "He is a skilled negotiator and an astute politician, but he knows nothing of war. His chambers are in the palace while I live amongst my men."

"It will be more of the same", Mourdagos predicted. Using his teeth, he tore at a loaf and swallowed it down with a gulp of wine.

Odovaker was in a thoughtful mood. "Before I came to live amongst the Romans, I believed them to be a race of aloof and haughty men and women who think themselves better than others. A warlike people, who, through decadence, excess and debauchery, have become soft. I viewed them like a wolf would a herd of cattle. When the pack is hungry, we would simply cross the borders into Roman lands and sate our hunger for violence and rapine."

"Have you changed your mind?" Abdarakos asked, a frown of confusion on his brow.

"No, warlord", Odovaker chuckled. "But I have come to believe that the tribes can learn much from Rome. There are many things that we can take from them that are not able to be loaded into the hull of a longship or the back of a packhorse."

"Like what?" Mourdagos asked.

"The way they record history on paper, or how to mill grain with the power of water", he said. "The secrets to building engines that can batter down stone walls. How to bring clean water to cities and cleanse the waste of thousands through sewers."

"How will the tribes ever learn to do that?" I asked, imagining Beremud and Kursik's disgust at digging sewers.

"If our warriors make homes for themselves amongst the Romans they will learn, even if it takes generations", Odovaker said.

"That is a noble goal", Mourdagos said. "But there is a more pressing problem."

"Which is?" Odovaker asked.

"To stop the Goths from doing that which you have described", the big man said. "Euric has already taken over most of Gaul. If you are not able to take control of the armies of the West, the Goths will. Then they will crush all the tribes that stand against them."

"I fear that you are right", Odovaker said. "I will do what I can and pray to the gods that Zeno returns to power."

He took a swallow from his cup. "Where will you go?" he asked Abdarakos.

"Ragnar and I will return to our people who live in exile amongst the Boat Heruli", the erilar said. "We will use the gold in our hull to raise spears and sail to the shores of Scandza with an army at our backs – an army strong enough to crush Othere, the Svear king who betrayed us."

"Then mayhap we can help each other", Odovaker said. "Now that Euric's Goths has been placated with gold, there is no war to fight other than the battle to keep my men content."

"And they will only be content if they are at war", Abdarakos replied, a smile forming on his lips.

"I will give you five hundred of my warriors to take north, warlord", Odovaker suggested. "The gold I receive in return will help to pacify the ones who remain behind. With a little help from Fortuna, I will be able to keep them content until Zeno regains his throne."

Abdarakos extended his arm and Odovaker gripped it in the way of the warrior, thereby concluding the arrangement.

* * *

That evening after I closed my eyes, I dreamt of Unni whom I had not seen for almost nine months.

Once more we walked hand in hand along the footpaths of the pine forest in the hills near Runaville. We strolled from the woods onto the green pastures that bordered the north of the village, and made our way towards the settlement.

Approaching the gate, I noticed that Svear spearmen guarded the entrance rather than Heruli oathsworn. Confused, I glanced at Unni to seek her counsel, but the love of my life had changed into Runa, the old Svear seer.

"Careful you must be, Iron One", she hissed. "Your path is not what it seems."

I must have frowned.

"A great upheaval is upon the world of man", she said. "The portents are everywhere", she added and gestured to a flock of birds circling overhead.

"What should I do?" I asked.

The old hag bent over at the waist and broke into a fit of laughter which must have lasted twenty heartbeats.

"Do what the gods want you to do", she replied when she had righted herself.

"I promised Unni that I would return by the fourth month of the new year", I said, which sounded like a pathetic excuse to my own ears. I averted my gaze in shame.

When I looked up, Unni had returned. She reached out and wrapped her arms around my neck her lips close to my ear. "Maybe you should learn to trust in the gods, Ragnar", she whispered.

* * *

Abdarakos clasped my shoulder, his grip like iron. "Wake up, Ragnar", he whispered into my ear. "There is trouble afoot."

In the flickering light of an oil lamp I noticed Mourdagos as well as Odovaker standing beside my bed. All wore their full armour, their blades strapped to their belts.

"During the hours of darkness, Orestes and his men have arrived at the gates of Ravenna with a thousand horsemen", Odovaker said while I donned my armour. "I am unsure of Orestes's intentions, but I believe that he is here to claim the purple."

"How many men do you have within the walls of Classe?" Mourdagos asked.

"Most of my men are stationed at the forts guarding the passes into Gaul", Odovaker said, his lips pursed. "I have less than eight hundred men who are fit to wield a blade. Almost half of them are patrolling the walls of Ravenna."

"Mayhap the best course of action is to do nothing", Abdarakos said. "Nepos is an incompetent. Orestes is not much different."

"There is one difference", Odovaker growled. "If Orestes claims the purple, he will be a usurper, a traitor, while Nepos, no matter how useless, has the backing of the East and the blessing of the senate."

"We should rescue Nepos", Odovaker said. "Orestes will kill him as soon as he breaches the walls of the city."

"We can use our ship", Mourdagos suggested.

Odovaker shook his head. "Orestes will expect Nepos to flee by ship", he said. "I have received reports that he has seized merchant ships. Already his men are patrolling the sea-walls of the city."

"There might be another way", I said.

"It is impossible to approach the city from the salt marshes", Odovaker sighed, his tone dismissive. "The bridges are controlled by Orestes. There is no way in."

"What seems impossible to one man may be not so difficult for another", I replied.

*　*　*

Less than half an hour later, guided by the light of the moon, we sailed through the channel that linked the lagoon with the Ionian Sea. We were not accosted, as Orestes had his hands full and cared little for merchants departing from the harbour at Classe.

Once we reached open water, we turned north. Five miles up the coast, Abdarakos leaned on the oar and the ship headed closer to the sandy beach. A hundred paces from the shore, Odovaker, Kauko and I lowered ourselves over the board into the cold water. To avoid suspicion, the ship did not throw anchor, but continued its northbound voyage.

We wore nothing but undyed tunics tied in with belts to which our daggers and waterskins were secured. In addition, each of us carried a bundle of dry clothes, tightly rolled up in sealskin and strapped to our backs.

"Orestes might have posted sentries on the beach", Odovaker said as we paddled closer to the shore.

"Do not be concerned", I replied.

Not long after, Odovaker and I staggered from the surf, dead tired.

Kauko, who swam like an otter, had reached the beach long before we had.

"Do you trust this man's skill?" Odovaker whispered.

"You will soon see for yourself", I replied.

When we reached the wild man's side, I noticed two bodies sprawled in the sand at his feet. "Sentries", he said, shrugged, and continued towards the hinterland.

Odovaker raised an eyebrow but issued no comment.

Shivering, we remained in the reeds at the edge of the estuary, waiting for the arrival of the grey pre-dawn.

When Kauko deemed that the light was sufficient, he rose from where he sat in a crouch. "Put your feet where I do", he said, and walked into the marshes.

The mudflats were a maze of reeds, mud and quicksand, crisscrossed by veins of narrow channels filled with water of varying depth. The water stank of decay. More than once did we pass corpses of men who had believed they could cross the mire. Kauko moved along as if he was strolling in the Roman Forum, only now and again did he pause and steal a glance at the faraway walls of Ravenna to get his bearings. Sometimes he came to a halt, scooped soil into a palm and rubbed it between his fingers, then proceeded to sniff it like a wolf would. Other times he plunged into a canal without pause. Each time we followed without question, sometimes wading through chest-high water for what felt like miles.

Late afternoon, when the sun was low in the sky, we finally arrived below the towering stone walls. It had taken almost a day to cross two miles of swampland, although we must have walked close to fifteen miles in total.

I realised then that I had never given scaling the wall any thought. "Can you climb it?" I asked Kauko.

"No", he replied.

I studied the defences. It was clear that the builders had known that no enemy would ever be able to assault the city from the swamps. The stonework was not of the same quality as the walls that faced the sea.

I noticed a lone sentry who patrolled the wall.

"Allow me", Odovaker said, and issued a shrill whistle.

The sentry's head jerked in our direction. Immediately he lifted his shield for protection against slingshot or arrows, raised his spear, and made his way along the rampart.

"Who goes there?" the man said when he noticed the three dark shapes standing knee-deep in the putrid water. He drew back his spear to skewer us.

"Get a rope and lower it, soldier", Odovaker growled.

"Lord?" the man asked and lowered his spear.

"Do you want me to stand here all day?" Odovaker said.

The spear and shield clattered onto the wall walk and the soldier trotted off. Sixty heartbeats later three men arrived. One carried a coiled rope.

* * *

"We should bathe first", I said as the duty centurion, a trusted man of Odovaker's, led the way to the palace.

"We have no time to waste on fripperies", Odovaker growled without slowing down.

"Nepos is an old-school Greek", I said. "Our appearance will carry much weight."

The Scirii prince came to a halt and regarded me and Kauko for five heartbeats, then his face morphed into a scowl. "You might have a point, Ragnar", he said. "You two look and smell like swineherds."

"As do you", I said, which caused him to smile.

* * *

An hour later, Odovaker and I were escorted into the presence of Julius Nepos. Both of us were dressed in simple white tunics. Around the Scirii prince's broad shoulders was draped a magnificent fur-edged crimson cloak befitting his status. Our hair and beards were neatly barbered and our bodies had been rubbed with sweet-smelling oils.

The emperor's gaze settled on me. He must have recognised me, but Nepos was no fool and he knew that his position was precarious to say the least.

"Have you come to gloat?" he asked Odovaker.

"No, lord emperor", he replied. "We have come to offer salvation."

With the wave of a hand the emperor dismissed the troop of attendants.

"I am listening, legate", Nepos said once the last of his people had left the chamber.

Odovaker gestured at me. "Ragnar and his people will take you across the Ionian Sea to Salona in Dalmatia", he said. "You will remain emperor, although you will live in exile."

"Why are you doing this?" he asked.

"To save Italia, lord", the Scirii prince replied.

To be continued...

Historical Note – Main Characters

Heruli and their companions

- **Ragnaris** is a Hun name with Germanic origins. He is a fictional character, following the journey of the Heruli through the fifth century AD.
- **Ildiko's** name is recorded in history. She was the bride of Attila and probably of Germanic origin.
- The Heruli family and friends of Ragnaris are all fictional. That includes **Abdarakos, Mourdagos, Kauko, Sigizan, Atakam, Leodis, Kursik, Boarex, Beremud** and **Asbadus**.
- **Rodolph** became the king of the Heruli during this time. It is not known who preceded him, but John the Deacon mentions that he was the last of their kings.
- Flavius Odoacer/**Odovaker**/**Ottoghar** was presumably a Scirii chieftain, who became a leading general in the West Roman foederati. He is mentioned as the king of the Heruli.

Romans

- **Leo the Thracian** was the East Roman emperor from 457 AD to 474 AD. It is said that he was a Bessian.

- **Flavius Zeno** was an Isaurian and reigned as Byzantine Emperor from 474 to 491 AD. (Albeit with a short interruption during 475/6 AD). His birth name was **Tarasis** Kodisa Rousombladadiotes.
- Flavius Ardabur **Aspar** was of Alanic-Gothic descent. From 424 AD until his death in 471 AD he was the real power behind the purple of the Eastern Roman Empire. He was an Arian Christian, and therefore not eligible to be emperor (some say that it was because he was of barbarian stock). **Ardabur** and **Patricius** were his sons.
- The name **Trokondas** is not fictional. Trokondas (or Trocundes) was an Isaurian general, famous in history with his brother **Illus**. Trokondas was often an ally of Zeno and often an enemy.
- **Sidonius Apollinaris** was a high born Roman and the bishop of Clermont. He was more than just a bishop and had a hand in organising the defences of the ailing Roman Empire in Gaul. Much of our knowledge of the history of this period relies on his writings.
- **Verina** was the wife of Leo I (The Thracian), the mother of **Ariadne**, the grandmother of **Leo II** and the sister of **Basiliscus** who seized power after Zeno was driven from Constantinople by a wave of anti Isaurian

riots, most probably instigated by Verina and her co-conspirators.

Men of the tribes

- **Attila** was the king or khan of the Huns.
- **Theodemir** was the king of the Ostrogoths and the father of **Theoderic the Great**.
- **Vidimir** was the brother of Theodemir, a king of a portion of the Ostrogoths. His son was also called **Vidimir**.
- **Geiseric** was the king of the Vandals, a Germanic tribe which, together with a grouping of Alans, conquered North Africa and established the Vandal Kingdom. Their ships caused havoc in the Mediterranean through piracy and coastal raids during the second half of the fifth century. It is said that he was a very clever and resourceful man.
- **Ferderuchus** and **Feva** (Feletheus was also known as Feva) were the sons of **Flaccitheus**, king of the Rugii. After Flaccitheus's death, Feva became king. Feva was married to an Ostrogoth woman by the name of **Gisa**, close family of Theodemir's.

- **Aldihoc** was the king of the Lombards during the middle of the fifth century AD. His son **Godehoc** succeeded him somewhere around 480 AD.
- **Euric** was the king of the Visigoths from 466 AD to 484 AD.
- **Childeric** was the king of the Franks during this period. He is believed to be the son of **Merovech**, father of the Merovingian dynasty.
- **Riothamus** was a Breton/British leader who fought against the Visigoths in Gaul. Some identify him with (the legendary?) King Arthur.

The Svear and Gautar

- **Unni** and **Runa** are fictional. They represent the Svear people and their agrarian culture.
- **Aun the Old** and his son **Egil** (Ogentheow) were legendary kings of the Svear.
- **Othere,** another semi-legendary king of the Svear, is said to have succeeded Egil.
- **Haecyn** and **Hygelac** were both legendary kings of the Gautar.

Historical Note – Storyline

The Heruli in Scandinavia

Archaeological evidence, especially the princely horse equipment found at Sösdala, indicate that during the fifth century AD, Eastern European horse warriors arrived on the shores of Scandinavia.

In his famous work, the *Heimskringla,* Snorri Sturluson tells of Odin, a great warlord, who arrived from the lands of the East. Snorri mentions that Odin was superior to the locals in many ways, and imparted his skills and customs. In later years, these early rulers were revered as gods.

I choose to believe that the Heruli (which had lived under Hunnic rule for long) were the ones responsible for the Eastern European influence. Their trek to Scandinavia is recorded by *Procopius*. It has been suggested that they settled amongst the people and became a military elite. The Scandinavian term *jarl* (equivalent to the British earl or duke) is said to be linked to the Heruli and the *erilaR* inscriptions found on elder futhark runestones.

* * *

There is much speculation about the nature of the relationship between the Svear and the Geats (Gautar), the two major tribes of the land which is called Sweden nowadays.

If indeed the Heruli settled in Scandinavia, it will, bar the unlikely discovery of ancient texts, never be clear how it happened.

I decided to incorporate elements of the poem "Beowulf" into the first part of the story. It is a well-known fact that the ones who record history does so in a way to enhances their own image. "What if Grendel were the good guy?" I asked myself...

The Balkans and the Pontic Steppes north of the Black Sea. (Lithuania, Belarus, Ukraine, Russia)

In later years the Varangian Guard, the personal guard of the Byzantine emperors, were primarily composed of warriors from Scandinavia. They travelled from their homeland along routes that are mentioned by ancient writers. I thought that it would be interesting for Ragnar and his companions to use the route along the Daugava and the Dnieper.

The Pontic Steppes north of the Black Sea (present day Ukraine) went through a stage of major upheaval during the fifth and sixth centuries AD. After the death of Attila and the fall of the Hun Empire, Proto-Bulgar tribes dominated these grasslands. During this period, the Avars (Var and Chunni), who were in turn fleeing from the Khazars (Astina clan of the Turks), entered the fray from the east.

The Avars are first mentioned by Priscus of Pannium in 463 AD as being in conflict with the Sabirs. The political landscape on the steppes was dynamic. Not only did tribes constantly move around, but they also changed loyalties and were often assimilated by other, stronger, tribes.

Based on genetic analysis of interred remains, it is believed that the noble elites of the Avars were ethnically different from the horde. It seems that the ruling class were of Mongolian origin.

Eastern Roman Empire

During the time covered by this book (474 to 476 AD), major upheaval took place in both the Eastern and Western Roman Empire.

- Leo the Thracian died early in 474 AD and was succeeded by Leo II, his five-year-old grandson who had been proclaimed as Caesar (heir apparent) by the ailing Leo I months before. The boy was the son of Leo I's daughter, Ariadne, and Zeno the Isaurian. Within weeks Zeno convinced the senate to appoint him as co-emperor.
- In early October 474 AD, Leo II died. There is much speculation around his death. Some believe that his mother poisoned him so that her husband could become sole emperor, while others believe that the boy's death had been faked.
- Verina decided to overthrow Zeno and place her lover, Patricius on the throne. The dowager empress attained the support of Basiliscus, her brother, who was a high-ranking general in the army.
- The conspirators instigated riots in the city, which forced Zeno to flee to Isauria early in 475 AD. He somehow managed to take the imperial treasury as well.
- Trokondas and his brother Illus followed Zeno to Isauria where they besieged him in a city.
- Meanwhile back at home, the conspirators fell out. Basiliscus, who had probably conspired with senators

behind Verina's back, arranged his own ascension to the purple. For good measure, he had Patricius, who was a possible rival, executed.
- Due to the empty treasury, Basiliscus had no funds to reward his supporters in the senate with. Soon he was forced to raise taxes. The riots continued and most of the Isaurians who remained in the city were slaughtered by the mob.

Western Roman Empire

- The Burgundian king, Gundobad, who succeeded Ricimer, the master of soldiers, appointed Glycerius as emperor in 473 AD. Leo the Thracian did not approve and he decided to send a possible rival to his own throne, Julius Nepos, to claim the Western throne.
- Nepos arrived in Rome in the middle of 474 AD, with an Eastern army at his back. Glycerius did not resist and was awarded with a senior office in the Roman Church in Dalmatia.
- Julius Nepos accomplished little. His armies were defeated by Euric of the Visigoths and he was forced to make peace and cede most of Roman Gaul to the invaders.

- In 475 AD Nepos appointed General Orestes as the master of soldiers. Orestes was a Roman patrician who served under Attila. Orestes soon revolted against the Greek emperor and Julius Nepos fled to Dalmatia.

Historical Note – Random Items

- A pierced gold *solidus* was found inside Othere's grave mount at Uppsala. The coin was minted in 476 AD. This was the inspiration for Abdarakos gifting Othere the gold coin.
- The Old Norse term, *hrosshvalr*, is believed to be the base of the word walrus. *Hrosshvalr* means horse-whale.
- The unnamed hunters I based on Tacitus's description of a people he referred to as *Fenni*.
- Do wolves kill only because they are hungry? I stumbled upon a newspaper article describing how wolves killed 120 sheep in a pasture in Dillon, Montana in August 2009. Almost all the carcasses were intact. The wolves first crippled the sheep and then ripped open their sides. Make up your own mind.
- The livestock dogs of the Vikings are said to have been the forefathers of the Dalbo dog, which became extinct around 1870. Dalbo dogs resemble the Leonberger breed. In 1833 a local Swedish priest wrote that his Dalbo dog had a bite like that of a crocodile. My theory is that they were related to the Kangal dogs of

the Steppes, that are known for their massively strong jaws.
- It is believed that chickens were first introduced to Scandinavia during the Bronze Age.
- In days of old, the people of the Steppes associated colours with direction. White was associated with the south.
- A *skeid* is a large longship with around thirty rowing benches.
- Beowulf can be translated to War-wolf or, some believe, Slaughter-wolf.
- I based Slaughter-wolf's helmet on the Coppergate helmet which dates to the eighth century. I have no doubt that similar helmets adorned the heads of earlier Anglo-Saxon mercenaries.
- The Dnieper (Deep River in Scythian) was known as the *Buri-Chai* during the period of Old Great Bulgaria (seventh century AD). *Burichai* has a nice ring to it and therefore I used it.
- *Zacharias Rhetor's Ecclesiastical History* refers to the lands between the Caspian Sea and the Black Sea as "*The land of Bazgun*". He mentions thirteen tribes occupying this area.

- During the time of this book, the Proto-Bulgars were migrating West to the area north of the Black Sea due to pressure from other tribes moving in from the East. *Theophilactus Simocatta* mentions, that when the Avars appeared in their lands, "*the Barsili, the Unogurs and the Sabirs were struck with horror ... and honoured the new-comers with brilliant gifts*".
- Perun (or Perkunas) and Volos (or Veles) are two major Baltic/Slavic gods. The battles between the two are believed to portray the ongoing struggle between the forces of good and evil. Some believe that Veles was not always seen as the evil one. He was a god of peasants while Perkunas was a god of the warrior elite.
- In ancient times seal hunters made their home on Ruhnu, the Island near the centre of the Bay of Riga.
- The Kurs (aka Curonians) were a tribe of warriors who, during the time of this book, inhabited the region that is today know as Western Latvia on the shores of the Baltic and the Bay of Riga.
- Longships under oar could travel at speeds of ten miles per hour and complete a sixty-mile-journey within a day. Less than sixty miles separate the Island of Ruhnu from the mouth of the Daugava.

- It is believed that (during the late fifth century AD) the upper reaches of the Daugava were under the control of Slavic (Sclaveni) tribes who were slowly migrating to the west under pressure from other tribes moving into the area from the east.
- Jews were not favoured by the rulers of fifth-century Byzantium. There were many laws that negatively impacted them, effectively relegating them to second-class citizens. Zeno's reaction when informed about the atrocities committed by the Greens were recorded by the Byzantine chronicler, John Malalas.
- One theory states that, in days of old, the Ural Mountains were called the "Stone Belt".
- In later years the Pechenegs (Turkish tribe) ruled the area bordering the north of the Black Sea. Apparently, there were eight clans. The clans were distinguished by the colour of their horses. There is no evidence that the Saragurs operated this way, although they are believed to be a Turkish tribe.
- Blue roan horses have coats that contain a mixture of black and white hair, giving them a blue appearance.
- According to a local legend, Kyiv was founded by three noble brothers and a sister, who, after their parents had been killed by eastern invaders, crossed to

the western bank of the Dnieper where they made a home for themselves.
- The Dnieper Rapids were seven sets of rapids in the river north of Zaporizhzhia, Ukraine. This famous wonder of nature was inundated by the Dnieper Reservoir in 1932 during the construction of the Dnieper Hydroelectric Station. Zaporizhzhia means *beyond the rapids*.
- In the time of Theodosius II it was illegal for Jews to be appointed to the civil service, although the law was apparently poorly policed. My inspiration for Jacob's father comes from a name mentioned in the ancient Jewish *Book of Medicines*. It is uncertain when Asaph lived, but it is estimated to be somewhere between the third and seventh century AD. Students of *Asaph ben Berakhyahu* were required to take an oath. The words that Jacob mumbles are adapted extracts from this oath.
- The modern table fork most probably originated in the Byzantine Empire prior to the fourth century AD.
- In his Natural History, Pliny the Elder suggests that, "*In cases where bread has stuck in the throat, the best plan is to take some of the same bread, and insert it in both ears.*"

- I have used the Notitia Dignitatum (Register of Dignitaries dated 400 AD) as the base for titles of functionaries used in this book.
- Some believe that the Colossus of Rhodes stood at the top of the hill overlooking the city rather than straddling the entrance to the harbour as depicted in later interpretations. The statue of the god Helios was constructed in 280 BC and stood for 54 years after which it fell down during a devastating earthquake. The Oracle of Delphi advised against rebuilding it so it remained on the ground for 800 years. Still, many travelled to see the remains of the colossal bronze and stone statue.

Historical Note – Place Names

Runaville (fictional name) – Area of Herrhamra, Sweden.

The Hall of Hrothgar – Near Lejre, Island of Zealand, Denmark.

The camp of the Boat Heruli – halfway between Hamburg and Lubeck, Germany. This is believed to be inside the ancient homeland of the Saxons, but there is a blurred line between them and the Heruli. Some believe that Herulians were part of the Saxons that invaded Britain.

The Home of the Kurs – Southern banks of the Bay of Riga, Latvia.

The Sclaveni town on the banks of the Daugava – Viciebsk, Belarus.

Smola on the Dnieper – A few miles downstream of Smolensk, Russia.

The place where Ragnar rescued three noble siblings – Kyiv, Ukraine.

The Dnieper Rapids – Between Dnipro and Zaporizhzhia, Ukraine.

The Island in the Dnieper where sacrifices were made – Khortytsia Island, Ukraine.

The City of Constantine – Constantinople, later Istanbul, Turkey.

Rhodos – Rhodes Island near the coast of Turkey.

Xanthos – Ancient town near Kas, Antalya Province, Turkey.

Melas River – Manavgat River near Side, Turkey.

Place of Fog – The Dumanli Spring that feeds the Manavgat River.

Attaleia – Antalya, Turkey.

Author's Note

I trust that you have enjoyed the fourth book in the **erilaR** series.

My aim is to be as historically accurate as possible, but I am sure that I inadvertently miss the target from time to time, in which case I apologise to the purists among my readers.

Kindly take the time to provide a rating and/or a review.

I will keep you updated via my blog with regards to the progress on the fifth book in the series.

Feel free to contact me any time via my website. I will respond.

www.HectorMillerBooks.com

Other books by the same author:

erilaR Series

- Part 1 – Stranger from Another Land
- Part 2 – Blood of the Khan
- Part 3 – War God from the Sea
- Part 4 – The Iron One

The Thrice Named Man Series

- Book I – Scythian
- Book II – Legionary
- Book III – Sasanian
- Book IV – Transsilvanian
- Book V – Goth
- Book VI – Roman
- Book VII – Illyrian
- Book VIII – Roxolani
- Book IX – Issedonian
- Book X – Herulian
- Book XI – Barbarian
- Book XII – Athenian

Printed in Great Britain
by Amazon